For my family—My wife Carrie, and my kids, Eric, Hannah and McKenna. And for my sister-in-law, Dolly. They all pitch in to keep our household from spinning wildly out of control, allowing me the time to write and draw and dream.

TRAPPED in
LUNCH LADY
LAND

DAVID M. SIMON

Children's Brains are Yummy Books
Dallas, TX

Trapped in Lunch Lady Land

Text Copyright © 2014 by David M. Simon

For more information, write:
CBAY Books
PO Box 670296
Dallas, TX 75367

Children's Brains are Yummy Books
Dallas, Texas
www.cbaybooks.com

Printed in the United States of America.

ISBN: 978-1-933767-35-2
ISBN: 978-1-933767-36-9 (ebook)

Table of Contents

1. The Secret Door 1
2. Batter Up. 10
3. Escape From the Ladle People 16
4. Saved by a Noodle. 24
5. You Want Fries With That? 30
6. Eddie Eggs. 37
7. The Skybeater. 45
8. Nacho Valley. 53
9. Ice Cream, You Scream 62
10. Who's Rescuing Who? 72
11. Canisaur 78
12. In the Belly of the Beast 88
13. Down the Drain. 99
14. The Great Lasagna Swamp 105
15. Eddie's Story. 114
16. The Catacombs 120

17. Get the Point 128

18. Caught in the Current 136

19. Clash of the Kitchenators. 145

20. One Bad Apple. 153

21. Reunion. 160

22. Pop Goes the Josh 166

23. Attack of the Lunch Ladies 173

24. Super Kuchen. 179

25. In Deep Jello. 188

26. Back to Normal? 195

CHAPTER 1

THE SECRET DOOR

"Hey, kid! You, with the red hair. Yeah, you! We've got a creamed corn emergency on our hands! Get down to the storeroom and fetch me a big can, quick now!" Lunch Lady Kuchen snarled at me from behind an empty steam table pan. She glared and waved a big, gloppy spoon in my direction.

I'm Josh Brannon, the kid with the red hair. I had cafeteria duty, on account of an incident involving a wad of chewing gum and Patty Anne McGinty's

1

chair, which I had almost nothing to do with, no matter what that tattletale Patty Anne said.

The truth was Mrs. Kuchen freaked me out. She prowled the lunch counter like a heavyweight boxer waiting for the bell to ring, her meaty hands balled into fists, her face bright red and sweaty. Her uniform had these weird stains on it that were never the same color as what we were eating that day. Plus her hairnet made her look like an alien. I didn't think she liked kids much.

Mrs. Kuchen barked, "Stop daydreaming, kid!" So I headed for the storeroom at the back of the kitchen.

The door opened with a creak, like the kind you hear in horror movies. Serling Heights Intermediate School was built back when my grandparents were kids, when Serling Heights, Ohio, had been just a village halfway between Cleveland and Pittsburgh. Then they kept adding on to the school, so now it looked like a bunch of different buildings stuck together.

Kind of like Frankenstein's monster. The cafeteria was in the oldest part of the school. The storeroom was about what you'd expect—cobwebs, damp stone walls, a sour, barfy smell. Yuck city.

I flicked on the lights and it didn't seem so bad, not that I was scared or anything. I mean, come on, I was almost twelve years old. A long flight of rickety metal stairs led down into the shadowy basement. Lunch Lady Kuchen screamed, "Move it!" and I took the steps two at a time.

It was cold down there, like I had descended a lot farther than fourteen steps. Rickety shelves lined the walls. Cans as big around as hubcaps filled the shelves, the labels faded and peeling. There were boxes of instant potatoes the size of tombstones. I found the corn on a bottom shelf at the far end of the storeroom, where the ceiling got lower and a big, greasy stain covered the floor. *Time for the Health Department to pay a visit*, I thought.

Something else caught my eye. In one corner,

half-hidden behind a cabinet that had sagged sideways under the weight of ancient pork n' beans, was a little wooden door. It looked way older than the school, which I knew was impossible. A sign on it read *KEEP OUT*. Underneath the sign someone had scratched a skull and crossbones into the wood, and beneath that *THIS MEANS YOU!* Now I had to see what was behind that door.

I dropped the canned corn and reached for the rusty handle. It turned, just barely, with a scraping metal sound. I pulled hard but nothing happened. I gritted my teeth, grabbed it with both hands and really yanked. Nothing. Just for the heck of it, I tried pushing instead of pulling, and the door cracked open an inch. That was all the encouragement I needed. I put my head down, dug my toes into the cracked floor, and leaned into it with my shoulder. Then two things happened simultaneously. A grinding squeal filled the basement. The door flew open, pulling me after it!

I tumbled through the air and landed with a plop in something soft and sticky. My body immediately began moving. I struggled to stand up, flailing my arms around. I was waist deep in a river of what looked like—mashed potatoes. No way.

Mom always said, "Josh will eat anything." I guess she's right, because I scooped up a handful and took a taste. Yuck! Not just mashed potatoes but instant mashed potatoes, the kind they serve in the cafeteria. The potatoes were lukewarm and runny, just like in school.

The current was surprisingly strong for something as thick as mashed potatoes, even runny instant ones. I really had to fight my way to the bank of the spud river. I climbed out, and my feet sank into the wet, brown ground. I thought I knew what it was, but there was only one way to be sure—I crouched down and took a big bite. Salisbury steak, the Wednesday special. Also lukewarm, of course. I guess we students can't be trusted with hot food.

I took a quick look around. I was no longer in the basement of my school, or anywhere in Serling Heights, that was for sure. This was big sky country, but the sky wasn't blue. It looked, and I knew this sounded stupid, like ceiling tile. From horizon to horizon, a big dome of ceiling tile. And instead of the sun shining down, an oversized fluorescent light fixture hung above me, flickering slightly.

The other thing I noticed right away was the smell. How do I explain it? Every once in awhile, our cafeteria served "Chef's Surprise." The surprise was that anyone ate it and lived to tell the tale. They took a week's worth of leftovers—meat, vegetables, bread, dessert and the odd used Band-Aid—and jumbled it all together in a toxic casserole.

We always knew when it was Chef's Surprise day. You could smell it cooking all over the school, even on the playground. Too many food scents that didn't belong together. Well, that was what this place smelled like. Gag.

I stood near a clump of bushes that just had to be giant carrot sticks. Down the shore was a grove of towering celery trees. "I sure hope this is a dream," I said out loud, surprised by the sound of my voice. "Nah, it can't be. Dreams don't smell this bad."

A loud popping sound and a bright flash of light made me look up. A person tumbled out of thin air and somersaulted into the river. This was getting weirder by the minute.

"Oh no!" I groaned. Patty Anne McGinty, bubblegum girl, sputtered to her feet. "Not her! Anyone but her!" Patty Anne wiped potatoes from her eyes and glared when she saw me on the riverbank.

"This is all your fault!" she screamed, wading toward me. She slipped and went under, then surfaced again. She shook her pigtails like a wet dog, flinging mashed potatoes in every direction. Patty Anne looked me right in the eyes and said, "I'm going to kill you." She's kind of scrawny, but she looked pretty serious, so I backed up a couple steps.

Patty Anne tried to climb up the bank but kept falling back in. I was busy keeping my distance. "Don't just stand there. Help me!" she yelled.

"First you're going to kill me, now you want my help. Which is it? And what are you doing here anyway?"

"Mrs. Kuchen asked me to check on you because you were gone so long. I poked my head through that little door and I slipped. Now get me out of here or else."

"Well, since you asked so nice." I grabbed one slimy hand and pulled her out, almost falling in myself. We sat at the edge of the river, breathing hard. Covered with potatoes, Patty Anne didn't look so prissy and perfect now.

She scowled at me. "What is this place? Is that river what I think it is?" She wrinkled her nose. "And what's that awful smell?"

"I have no idea what this place is, and yep, that's an instant mashed potato river. You'll get used to the smell, after your nostrils go numb. At least, I hope so. And check this out." I pried up a chunk of ground and popped it in my mouth. "Salisbury steak."

"Oh, gross!" Patty Anne looked like she might throw up, which was a bonus for me.

My stomach growled, and I realized I had missed lunch. I scooped up another handful of Salisbury steak. Just then, something whizzed past my ear and smashed into the ground, splashing us with gravy. It was a Tater Tot as big as my head. Another hit right at Patty Anne's feet, almost knocking her down, then another, and another. We were being bombarded with giant Tater Tots!

CHAPTER 2

BATTER UP!

We dove behind the carrot-stick bushes. The tots came from across the river. I peeked around and saw three big ladles with skinny little arms and legs and mean little faces. They had to be at least ten feet tall and stood next to a huge stockpile of Tater Tots. They tossed them up into the scoops of their ladles and flung them in our direction, like catapults.

With each Tater Tot that landed near us, they jabbered at each other and did a little dance. Their aim was pretty good. Soon they began hitting the bush we were hiding behind. The tots were frozen, as hard as rocks. The bush shook dangerously with each hit. We were cornered!

Patty Anne snuck a look. "Great. A mashed-potato river, Salisbury-steak mud, and now giant ladle people throwing food bombs at us. And you. I hate this place." She made a face in my direction. "This is still all your fault."

"Yeah, well, you can yell at me later, after we get away from these creeps." The carrot stick bush we hid behind gave me an idea. Keeping my head as low as I could, I reached up and snapped off a branch as long as a baseball bat. "Hey, Patty Anne, how are you in the batter's box?" I played third base and clean-up hitter on the Serling Heights travel team.

"Better than you."

"I doubt it." I knew Patty Anne was on the girls' travel team, but come on, who was she kidding?

"You are such a jerk!"

"Then prove it. Grab yourself a bat and let's see

11

how good these ladle people are in the field."

Patty Anne broke off a branch. She nibbled around one end of her bat.

"This is not the time for a snack!" I yelled.

She swallowed a mouthful of carrot and gave me the evil eye. "If you must know, I'm tapering the bat so it's easier to hold. I suggest you do the same." She went back to work.

Actually, it was a pretty good idea. As I munched away on my own bat, I caught her smug smile out of the corner of my eye. "Are you ready, princess?" I asked.

"Shut up and let's do this," she said through clenched teeth.

"Batter up!" We jumped out from behind the bush. I got into my batting stance and took a couple of practice swings—the carrot bat felt pretty good.

I took a whack at the next Tater Tot that came my way, but it hooked off to the side. Foul tot. I connected on the next one, and it landed with a plop in the spud river. The ladle people started to look confused.

I misjudged the next one completely. It was a brushback pitch, way inside. I jumped back, and it caught me on the foot. I dropped my bat and hopped up and down in pain.

Patty Anne was busy hitting solid line drives. "Hey, you going to dance around all day or get back to batting practice?"

"Be quiet," I muttered. Now it was personal. I started to really knock the tots out of the park. I smacked a nice one that hit the ladle people's stockpile, causing a mini avalanche. That made them mad. They jumped up and down and shrieked in our direction.

Patty Anne caught a Tater Tot right on the carrot stick's sweet spot and slammed it booming across the river. It caught one of them right in the scoop. The ladle person spun around, off balance, and fell over, landing hard on its mean little butt.

Patty Anne whooped, "Home run!" and high-fived

me. Then she seemed to remember that she hated me and quickly dropped her hand. The other two ladle people shook their fists at us and bent down to help their friend.

Now's our chance, I thought, and looked around for a way to escape. Behind us was a high Salisbury steak ridge that went on in both directions as far as I could see. Climbing that mushy wall of meat was out. I spied the celery trees. Perfect!

"Patty Anne, this way!" While the ladle people were still busy with their fallen buddy, we sprinted to the trees. I felt a little safer surrounded by the big celery stalks.

"You really pounded that Tater Tot, Patty Anne. Nice shot. For a girl."

"For a girl? For a girl? I'll show you what a girl can do—" She came at me, fists raised.

I backed away, holding up my hands. "Relax. I was just kidding. That was a solid hit, for anyone. Look, we need to work together. Truce?"

She gave me a fierce look, then smiled, just a little. She dropped her hands. "All right, truce. If you can stop being a jerk for a little while."

"I'll do my best, but it's going to be tough. You seem to bring out the jerk in me."

"It's a gift. By the way, thanks for pulling me out of the river. Even if I am only here because of you." She just had to get that little dig in, but oh well. Patty Anne looked down at herself with an expression of disgust. Just like me, she was covered head to toe in mashed potatoes and gravy. She tried to wipe away some of the gunk but soon gave up. She stamped her foot, which only splashed her more. "This is going to get really old. I hope there's some water around here somewhere."

"Yeah, well, right now we need to get past our friends there and there's no way we can climb that." I pointed at the ridge. "Any ideas?"

Patty Anne looked thoughtfully at the trunk of a celery tree. "Yes, as a matter of fact. Give me a hand."

CHAPTER 3

escape from the ladle people

"Remember the dugout canoes we learned about in American history?" Patty Anne asked.

"I'm way ahead of you."

We jumped up as high as we could and grabbed hold of either side of one of the celery stalks. We shimmied higher and higher, until the celery snapped off at the ground with a sharp crack. I landed on my shoulder, but the soft ground cushioned my fall, even if it did cover me in more gravy. Patty Anne landed flat on her rear end.

We had a big piece of celery roughly the size and shape of a dugout canoe. The top end even curved up, just like a real canoe. The snapped-off end was another story. I dug up a big chunk of Salisbury steak and wedged it into the gap to plug it up, then finished it with a layer of mashed potatoes. The way I figured, if the potatoes tasted like plaster, they might work like plaster. It would just have to hold. Now we needed protection from the Tater Tots. One more trip up a stalk and we had a roof.

It only took a minute to drag the two halves down to the river's edge. The ladle people were back at it, so we had to duck and weave. I pushed the bottom of the canoe halfway into the river, and we crawled in, dragging the top half after us. The second stalk had been a little thinner, so it was a nice snug fit on top.

"Okay, start rocking," I said.

"Stop giving me orders!" Patty Anne snapped. "I know what to do. It was my idea, remember?" Touchy, touchy.

We rocked back and forth until the canoe slid into the river. I held my breath, waiting to see if the current would carry us, if the meat plug would hold, or if we were going to sink.

"I think it's working," Patty Anne whispered, like she was afraid a loud voice would dunk us. I wasn't concerned about it. We sailed a spud river in our celery canoe, trying to escape from giant ladle people. It seemed a little silly to worry about making too much noise.

Tater Tots made dull, wet thudding sounds as they landed all around us. Wham! The first direct hit shook the canoe, but the roof held. A potato wave splashed over the front and Patty Anne quickly bailed with both hands. A couple more good splats hit the canoe before we sailed out of range.

We could no longer hear the hooting and grumbling of the ladle people, and the tots stopped landing near us.

"I think we're safe," Patty Anne said.

"Cool. Let's have a look around. If that's okay with you," I added with just a little sarcasm. We heaved the top off the canoe. It hit the river with a loud *plop*, then bobbed away.

We were sailing through a spaghetti jungle. Huge spaghetti trees crowded the shore of the river and tangled together above our heads. It was much darker here ... the fluorescent sun barely penetrated the noodle canopy. Curly pasta vines as big around as my arm dangled over the river, dripping tomato sauce. In fact, tomato sauce oozed from the spaghetti branches, like sap from trees. Meatballs the size of pumpkins hung in bunches. "This is one freaky place," I said.

Patty Anne took a big bite of our canoe. "At least we won't go hungry," she said between chews.

"I hate celery. And stop eating our boat out from under us."

"It's good for you," Patty Anne said with an I-know-more-than-you smile.

"Well, duh, that's why it tastes so bad. You're not

much fun at parties, are you?" The girl really pushed my buttons.

Strange, metallic chattering filled the air. "What is that?"

Patty Anne pointed straight up. "There!" Dozens of strange little creatures swung through the trees. It looked like someone had swiped a bunch of forks from the cafeteria, smuggled them into metal shop, and soldered them together into little monkey robots. They had thin, spiky arms and legs and long, springy tails. Swinging from noodle to noodle with hands, feet, and tails, the forkmonkeys stayed above us, screeching while we floated down the river.

Patty Anne put her hands over her ears. "Oh man, that's worse than nails on a blackboard." One of the creatures picked a meatball and dropped it, just missing us. They all howled louder. "I think they're laughing at us."

I was paying so much attention to the forkmonkeys, it took me a minute to notice that we were picking up speed. Pretty soon they couldn't keep up with us and we left them behind. Excellent, I thought. They were giving me a headache.

It was finally quiet. "So what do you think this place is?" I asked.

Patty Anne looked thoughtful. "It has something to do with the cafeteria, I'm sure about that. The door was there for a reason, and just about everything here seems to be made of cafeteria food." She dipped a finger in the river, tasted a dollop of potato, and made a face like she had just stepped in dog poop. "I don't even like cafeteria food."

"Aw, it's not so bad. Say, Patty Anne. I have a question to ask you, but promise not to laugh."

"I'll try."

"Yeah, okay. So here's the question. Did you ever notice anything weird about Mrs. Butterbean, our old lunch lady, and Mrs. Kuchen?"

"Yes!" she screamed, nearly knocking me out of the canoe. "It's like they're the same person but different!"

She paused and frowned. "It sure sounds stupid when you say it out loud."

"No, no. That's exactly it. My friends think I'm two tacos shy of a combination plate, but that's what I think too. I mean, Lunch Lady Kuchen might be a little more hulking, and their faces aren't that similar, but it's like her and Butterbean came from the same basic mold .... I hate it when something makes sense inside your head but not when it comes out of your mouth."

"Maybe we're onto something here. Or maybe we're both a couple of tacos light."

For the first time since I had arrived, I felt relatively okay. It even smelled better here in the spaghetti jungle, kind of like my friend Rudy Bennaducci's house. Rudy's grandma lived with him, and spent all her time cooking incredible meals. I would happily marry Grandma Bennaducci if she would make me homemade cavetelli every day.

I lay back in the canoe, hands behind my head,

and closed my eyes. I tried to ignore where we were for a while, enjoying the gentle rocking of our celery boat. That enjoyment was short-lived, however, because Patty Anne's annoying chirp of a voice forced me to open my eyes and sit up.

"Josh!" Patty Anne nudged me with her foot. "Listen!"

"What? What?"

"Listen!"

I heard it then. We looked at each other and said it together: "Waterfall!"

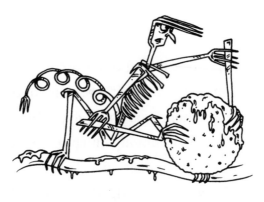

CHAPTER 4

SAVED BY A NOODLE

The thick thunder of mashed potatoes splashing over the falls grew louder. We sailed around a bend in the river and there it was, dead ahead. I mentally added canoeing to the top of my list of things I was going to give up if I ever got back home.

"Well, Patty Anne, you have to admit this place is never boring." I was trying to be funny, but I was starting to sweat.

"Nope, not boring at all." She looked as scared as I felt. "Now what?"

"See that big bunch of spaghetti vines hanging low over the falls? If we can jump up and grab hold, we might be able to pull ourselves to safety."

"Might be able to?"

"Hey, you got any better ideas? The falls are coming up quick," I yelled over the roar.

"We could try jumping in and swimming for it. It's not that deep."

"No way," I said. "The current's too strong. We'll get swept down the falls."

"Yeah, I think you're right. Okay, spaghetti vines it is. I guess we better stand up."

Roast beef boulders stuck up out of the potatoes, and we banged between them like a pinball. We shakily got to our feet. The canoe jerked sideways as we stood up and Patty Anne nearly went over the side. I grabbed her hand to steady her. She yanked it away and got her feet back under her. "I can do this!"

she said. "I'll see you up there."

The spud falls were only a few feet away. I took a deep breath and bent my knees. "This is it! One! Two! Three!" We jumped as the front of the canoe crossed the edge of the falls.

I snagged an armful of spaghetti. The pasta stretched a little, but it held. I caught a glimpse of Patty Anne lunging for a vine, then my left hand hit a patch of sauce and I started to slide. I stopped myself by hooking a leg in a loop of spaghetti. I couldn't see Patty Anne anywhere.

"Patty Anne!" I screamed. "Where are you?" I looked down, afraid of what I might see as our canoe tumbled down the falls.

"Josh, behind you!"

Not good. Patty Anne dangled below me with her fingers dug into a single strand of spaghetti. She swayed back and forth, her legs loose and hanging over the lip of the falls. There were no other noodles within reach.

"Well," she said, "things could be worse. At least I didn't go over the falls." I knew she was trying to be tough, but her voice was shaking and her face had gone pale.

"How long can you hold on?"

"Um, I don't know. Not real long." Her knuckles started turning white.

I already had one leg hooked in a spaghetti loop. If I could get the other leg in there, I might be able to swing down and reach her. It was worth a shot. "Patty Anne, I'm going to try something. Hang on."

I adjusted my grip, wrapping my arms tightly around a tangle of pasta branches. My right leg hung free. I heaved it up and over the loop. So far, so good. *Just like the monkey bars at school*, I told myself. I held my breath and let go with my hands. My body swung down, and I bounced a little, but my knees were hooked solidly.

I looked at Patty Anne's now upside-down face and said, "We've got to stop meeting like this."

"Ha ha. You're a funny guy." Sweat beaded on her forehead. I had to hurry.

I stretched my arms out as far as I could reach, but she was still at least a foot away. I started swinging, getting a little closer each time. My fingers brushed her hands. Next time, I thought, here we go.

My fingers closed around her wrists. "Let go of the vine!" I yelled. Patty Anne swung free. The spaghetti we both hung from sagged, but it held.

Patty Anne hauled herself up hand over hand, using my body and a pasta branch. She found a good perch, then reached down and pulled me up to a sitting position.

We were both safe. I felt weird inside, like I needed to laugh and cry and maybe throw up, all at the same time.

Then Patty Anne turned her back to me. "I'm still mad at you," she said. "This doesn't let you off the hook. Thank you for saving me, but it's still your fault I'm here in the first place."

I felt my face burning. "Are you kidding? You were about to fall! You—whatever." Patty Anne didn't say anything, and I didn't know what to say. Now she was the one being a jerk. Here I had thought we were starting to make a pretty good team. Never mind. "Come on. Let's climb a little higher."

When I finally looked down through a break in the spaghetti, the bottom of the falls seemed a mile away. I had to close my eyes because the view made me dizzy.

CHAPTER 5

YOU WANT FRIES WITH THAT?

We kept climbing. I now had a coat of tomato sauce on top of the mashed potatoes and gravy. This was one messy place. Occasionally we heard fork-monkeys clattering in the distance, but we never saw them again.

Patty Anne swung by on a vine, like a goopy Tarzan. Or maybe Jane. She was laughing. "This is fun!" Her mood swings were giving me whiplash, but I liked happy Patty Anne better.

"Hey, look there. I think we're above the level of the Salisbury steak ridge. Let's head that way."

"Why not? It's been at least an hour since something tried to kill us."

Funny girl.

We passed the top of the ridge and began climbing down. The tangles of spaghetti were easy to crawl through, but I did get stuck a couple of times. Once a noodle wrapped around my leg so tightly I couldn't get it out. I did the only thing I could think of—I ate through it. Not bad. Al dente, I think they called it. I had a handful of meatball to go with the pasta. It was a little mushy and overcooked, but I'd had worse.

The pasta branches thinned out as we made our way lower. I could see glimpses of the ground below, a golden field of tall grass waving in the breeze. "Finally, something normal," I said.

"Don't be so sure. This place is full of surprises."

"You're right about that." I hung from the lowest loop of spaghetti and dropped, landing with a crunching sound.

Patty Anne dropped down next to me. "Grass isn't crunchy," she said, pulling up one of the fat blades. She sniffed it, smiled, and took a big bite. "But french fries are!" We stood in a field of two-foot-tall french fries that went on as far as we could see. In my opinion, french fries were one of the main food groups. These were beautiful, perfectly golden brown and crusty with salt. I picked one and took a big chomp—delicious!

"Hey, what gives?" I asked. "I thought you only eat stuff that's good for you. French fries definitely do not qualify."

"Okay, so you found my one weakness. French fries are my kryptonite. I don't care how bad they are for me."

"Wow, there's actually a real kid somewhere inside you," I said. "We're making progress."

"Shut up," Patty Anne mumbled, her mouth full.

The ground was harder here, not so soupy. I kicked up a small chunk and braved a nibble. Old meatloaf. The air here had a slightly greasy smell that was only a little unpleasant. I could see low hills off in the distance—and something else. I shaded my eyes and pointed in that direction. "Do you see what I see? Unless I'm nuts, that's a log cabin, with smoke coming out of the chimney."

Patty Anne swallowed a mouthful of fry and looked where I pointed.

"Yep, that's a cabin all right. Who, or what, do you think lives there?"

I shrugged. I had no guess. "Let's find out."

We set off in that direction, munching french fries as we went. The fluorescent sun warmed my back. The various foods coating my body began to dry and crack. I peeled off chunks as we walked. The stink was so bad it was almost visible. Patty Anne tried to scrape her hair clean, but she wasn't having much luck. It looked like she had dreadlocks.

Something had been bothering me. "Patty Anne, I want you to know I didn't put that gum on your chair. It was Tim Connelly."

"I know."

"You know? Then why did you rat me out?"

She stopped and faced me. "Because you saw him do it, and you didn't tell me. That's just like doing it yourself in my book. Besides, those were my favorite jeans, and they got completely ruined. I was mad."

"I'm sorry. It's just that you're always so perfect. You get straight As. Your clothes are never messy. You're good at sports. You don't get in trouble. I bet you've never had a detention!"

Patty Anne's eyes were wet. "Is that so bad? Yes, I like to look nice. But I work really hard for those straight As. I study all the time, and sometimes it's a real pain. I have an older sister who's Miss Perfect. No matter how good I do, my parents compare me to her. You think I'm too perfect, they think I'm not perfect enough. I can't win!"

This should have made me feel bad, but I guess I was still ticked off about her attitude back at the falls. I had saved her skinny butt and she hadn't even thanked me! "You know what?" I yelled. "It was just a little joke. Get over yourself and grow a sense of humor. When we get back, I'll buy you some stupid new jeans!"

"It's got nothing to do with the jeans! You are so thick!" Patty Anne started walking again. "If you don't get it, I'm not going to explain it to you. Just forget it."

"I don't understand girls!" I screamed to the ceiling tile sky.

"You don't understand anything," she said in a near whisper and kept on walking. I guess she had me there.

As we got closer to the cabin, we came across paths in the french fry field where the fries had been beaten down. We followed one that headed in the general direction of the cabin. I started to feel like we weren't alone any more, like we were being followed.

I stopped, and I swore I could hear a faint rustling in the fries. "Do you hear that?" I whispered.

"What?"

"Listen." We both froze.

"Yeah, something's moving in the field. Let's get going."

I tried to shake off the prickly feeling on the back of my neck as we kept walking.

The closer we got to the cabin, the weirder it looked. It was built like a log cabin, but those weren't logs. "Hotdogs," I finally said. "Enormous hotdogs."

"Why not?" Patty Anne muttered.

The hotdog cabin had a roof of french fries tied in bundles and stacked closely together. A big, circular area around the cabin had been smooshed flat. We stopped a hundred feet away, searching for signs of life. The feeling of being followed was stronger than ever, but I couldn't see anyone. Then I heard a voice.

"Hey, kid! You, with the red hair. Yeah, you! Could you give me a hand?"

CHAPTER 6

eDDIe eGGS

The head of a boy around my age poked up out of the ground. At least, that's how it looked at first. As we got closer, I realized he was climbing out of a hole.

The kid had a rope around his shoulders. The rope was attached to a sled made from a slice of burnt toast the size of, well, a sled. Lashed to the sled was a big pile of those three-foot-long hotdogs. The hole was dug at a steep angle, and the kid was half-way out, struggling with the weight.

Patty Anne and I each grabbed one of his hands

and helped pull him the rest of the way out. He slipped out of the rope and bent over, trying to catch his breath.

"Thanks," he said between gasps. "I guess this load was one wiener too many."

He straightened up and looked us over. "Wow, you guys are a mess. Lunch Lady Land will do that to you." The kid was grimy but relatively gravy-free. He wore beat up jeans and a crusty T-shirt. Matted blonde hair hung in his eyes.

Patty Anne said, "Lunch Lady Land? What's Lunch Lady Land?"

"And who are you?" I added.

"Oh, sorry. You two are probably freaked out seeing another human here. I don't see a whole lot of people, and I guess my manners are a little rusty. I'm Eddie Kowalski, but you can call me Eddie Eggs."

We introduced ourselves. Eddie started walking toward the door of his hotdog house and waved for us to follow. "Come on in, and sit down. You're probably tired. Not hungry, though, I bet. Nobody ever goes hungry here."

Patty Anne and I looked at each other and shook our heads, but we followed.

The inside of Eddie's home was as weird as the rest of Lunch Lady Land. Everything, and I mean everything, was made from some kind of food. There was a couch built from the same celery we had used for our canoe. Chicken nuggets made great little tables. A marshmallow served as a beanbag chair, and several more smooshed together formed a bed. He had used carrot sticks like two-by-fours, constructing cabinets and a worktable. I was totally impressed.

As we sat down on the couch, I said, "Eddie, this is amazing."

He actually blushed a little. "Well, thanks. Lunch Lady Land does tend to bring out your creativity."

Patty Anne got right to the point. "Eddie, what exactly is Lunch Lady Land? Besides sloppy and dangerous, I mean."

"This isn't going to make a whole lot of sense, but here goes. This is the place where all lunch ladies come from. They're created here, they train here, and then they end up in school cafeterias all over the world."

"Created?" Patty Anne rocked forward so fast she nearly tipped the celery couch. "What do you mean, 'created?'"

"Have you ever noticed how lunch ladies look like each other? Not exactly alike, but similar? It's not a coincidence."

Patty Anne and I both blurted out, "Aha!" She shot me a dirty look.

"Best as I can figure it, this is some kind of alternate universe. Or something. The lunch ladies won't tell me. I have no idea how it works. And believe me, I've had time to think about it."

"How long have you been here?" Patty Anne looked worried.

"What year is it?" Eddie asked.

"2014."

"I can't believe it's been that long," Eddie said. His eyes clouded over, and he seemed to forget we were there for a minute. Eddie shook his head, then continued. "Friday, September 13, 1975. I had cafeteria duty. I was carrying a tray of pudding cups, and I slipped in some grease. Down I went. Pudding everywhere. Lunch Lady Boullion was so mad, I swear I could see steam rising off her red face. I got down on my hands and knees to pick up the cups, and saw that one had rolled behind the fryer. When I crawled back there to get it, I noticed a little red button in the wall. A metal plate over the button said, *DO NOT PUSH!* Hey, I'm only human! I pushed. The floor dropped open like a trap door and here I am."

"Thirty-nine years? That's impossible!" Patty Anne shouted. "You can't be much older than we are."

"That's the other crazy thing about Lunch Lady Land. Time is broken here. I had just turned twelve when I got here and I haven't aged a day. My hair doesn't grow. My nails don't grow."

41

I didn't know what to say as I let that roll around in my head, so I changed the subject. "Why do you call yourself Eddie Eggs?" I asked.

"Actually that's what the lunch ladies call me." He stood up. "Come on outside and I'll show you."

We sat in a circle in front of the cabin. Eddie put two fingers in the corners of his mouth and whistled. I'd always been embarrassed that I couldn't do that. Anyway, the french fries at the edge of the clearing immediately began to shake. I tensed up, ready for anything. Patty Anne looked like a runner at the starting line.

Eggs poured out of the fry field from all directions. Big eggs, at least two feet tall. They came at us, spinning like tops, bumping into each other and purring. Yep. Purring. They surrounded us and moved in close, gently pushing against our shoulders, purring like little round, white motorboats.

Eddie spread his arms wide, and eggs crowded in. "Patty Anne and Josh, these are my friends, the eggs."

"But what are they exactly?" I asked, petting one of them. Its purr was strangely soothing.

"I don't really know. They're just the eggs. They keep me company and I protect them. That's why the lunch ladies let me stay here."

"Wait a minute!" Patty Anne squeaked. She cleared her throat, then started again. "You can leave if you want? You're staying here on purpose?"

"The eggs need me. Nobody back in the world needs me, or wants me, for that matter."

I could tell by the tone in his voice, and the way he hung his head as he talked, that this was a sore subject for Eddie, but I didn't think Patty Anne realized it. She kept pushing. "Don't you miss your family? Your friends? Your parents must be worried sick!"

Eddie hugged the eggs close. When he finally spoke, his voice was under control, but just barely. "Look. There's nothing and no one for me back there. Let's leave it at that for now, okay?"

Patty Anne looked down, her face red. "Okay. But does

that mean we can leave Lunch Lady Land?"

Eddie seemed glad to talk about something, anything, else. "It's complicated from what I hear, but sure, the lunch ladies can help you. You have to get to them, though, and that's not so easy." Eddie jerked his head up, like he had heard something. The eggs stopped purring and began spinning in place.

Eddie said, "Come and help me!" He ran to the hotdog sled and grabbed the rope, heading for the back of the cabin. We joined in. The eggs nervously wobbled along with us. They looked scared, which is hard to do without a face.

"Eddie, what is it? What's wrong?" Patty Anne asked.

"It's coming." Behind the cabin stood what looked like a huge slingshot planted in the ground. Eddie had bound together several lengths of celery for strength. The rubber-band part of the slingshot was a gigantic wad of stretched-out chewing gum. We added the wieners to a stockpile already stacked next to the slingshot.

Now I was getting scared. "What's coming?"

"The skybeater!"

CHAPTER 7

THE SKYBEATER

I heard it then, a high whirring sound in the distance. Like metal vibrating against metal. A speck appeared just below the ceiling tile sky. It headed straight at us, moving fast. Way too fast.

"Oh man, it's big," said Patty Anne as it got closer. "And not very friendly looking."

Not friendly looking. That was an understatement. The skybeater looked like a giant eggbeater crossed with one of those killer fighting robots. It flew like an upside down helicopter, the whirling, razor-sharp beater blades slicing through the air. Fluorescent sunlight flashed off the metal. Beady red eyes glowed above the blades. Where the blade shafts met the body, there was a ragged round mouth with more teeth than a T-Rex.

"How does that thing fly?" Patty Anne said. "It breaks every law of physics."

"I don't think it cares about physics." I had to raise my voice. The closer the skybeater got, the louder the noise. It sounded like a chef at one of those Japanese steak houses clanging his knives together. Not a comforting thought.

"It doesn't care about anything," Eddie said, "except attacking whatever it feels like. And it really loves to scramble eggs. That's why I have to stay here." Eddie patted the tops of the eggs closest to him. "Come on, it's almost here. Help me load a missile." We fitted a hotdog into the sling pocket and walked it back, stretching the gum tight.

"Wait a minute!" Patty Anne shouted over the

racket. "We're going to fight off that metal monster with … wieners?"

"Hey, they're big wieners," I said, trying to be reasonable. The truth is I was a little worried myself. Okay, a lot worried.

Eddie took careful aim. "It's the best weapon I've found. The hotdogs have just the right sludgy consistency, so if you hit the skybeater with enough of them it gunks up the blades. If the blades slow down too much, it can't stay up. The skybeater is at its most lethal in the air; it doesn't have as much control on the ground. Okay, here we go! Let 'er rip on three. One—two—three!"

We released the sling, and the hotdog flew through the air with surprising speed. Blam! Direct hit on the right beater blade. The missile burst on impact, showering the skybeater with meat by-products. A strong hotdog stench filled the air, like when you microwave one too long and it explodes. The monster screeched and veered away.

I slapped Eddie on the back and we high-fived. "Nice shot!"

"Great aim," Patty Anne said. "You must get a lot of practice."

"Yeah, the skybeater pays us a visit every couple of weeks. I spend a lot of time in the hotdog mine, digging up more ammo. Now let's load up. It's coming around for another run!" The big creep wheeled around and streaked in low, weaving back and forth so it was harder to hit.

We quickly put another missile in the sling and pulled back. As the skybeater swooped into our sights, lined up between the slingshot uprights, we launched. The hotdog shot forward, but the skybeater dodged at the last moment, and the missile glanced off the side without doing any damage.

The monster churned straight at us. The eggs scattered and the three of us dove for cover. The ground shook and a horrible grinding sound filled the air as the blades hit where we had been standing a second before. A geyser of ground meat spewed up and rained down on us. I guess the meat was dry enough that it didn't clog the blades like hotdogs. The skybeater soared away. It left behind a ragged crater four feet across and at least two feet deep.

We scrambled to our feet and loaded another dog. My knees felt like jelly. I glanced over at Patty Anne and was surprised to see that she didn't look scared. She looked furious. "That's it," she muttered under her breath, "you're going down, you oversized kitchen appliance."

So much for prim and proper. "Where'd that come from?" I asked.

"I'm just pretending it's you," she said.

I guess I had that coming.

"Besides," Patty Anne said. "I'm tired of getting pushed around in Lunch Lady Land. It's time to fight back!"

Eddie said, "All right! Let's do it!" The skybeater swung around for another pass. We got it in our sights and let go. The hotdog smashed Metalhead right between the eyes and it wobbled in the sky.

We found our rhythm: Load, aim, fire. Load, aim, fire. We kept it off balance, not giving it a chance to attack. Pulverized meat coated the skybeater. Hotdog casings tangled around the rotors. It howled and bucked in the air. Smoke trailed from its mouth.

My arms were just about dead. I had trouble breathing. Patty Anne was bent over, catching her breath in ragged gulps. Eddie wasn't even winded. "Keep it up, guys. The skybeater's getting pretty slimed. It'll give up soon."

As he said that, the skybeater lurched. The beaters sputtered, stopped, caught again. It seesawed to the ground like a bird with a broken wing, landing hard. The skybeater clearly wasn't dead, but it lay there, groaning. We kept our distance. Eddie said, "Wow, I think it stuck around too long." The eggs rolled out from various hiding places.

"Now what?" Patty Anne whispered.

"I have no idea. This has never happened before. It always flies away while it still can."

As he said that the beaters roared to life. It shot forward, wobbling out of control, grinding up ground like the Tasmanian Devil. "It was faking!" I yelled.

We scattered. So did the eggs, but it caught one out in the open. I heard Eddie scream, "Noooo!" as the egg shattered between the beaters, its inside egg stuff splashing all over. The metal monster zigzagged off toward another egg.

I caught movement out of the corner of my eye. It was Patty Anne on a dead run for the skybeater. I yelled for her to stop, but she ignored me, as usual. Her face was bright red; her teeth bared. I'd never seen a human being so ticked off. I wouldn't want to be in that monster's shoes.

Patty Anne leaped onto the skybeater's back, right behind the blades. I had no idea what she was going to do. I don't think she did either. She shook her fists. "Don't you dare scramble another egg!" Then she punched it right in its little red eyeball.

The skybeater did not look amused. I doubted it ever looked amused. It spun and bounced, trying to shake her off. Patty Anne clung there like a champion bull rider.

"Hang on!" I screamed for the second time that day. It was getting to be a habit. She was still incredibly annoying, but I had to admit it was a crazy brave thing to do. Stupid, but brave.

The skybeater leaped into the air and began to gain altitude. "Eddie, what's it doing?" I screamed.

It was already too far away to see clearly. I couldn't make out Patty Anne any more.

"It's heading home. To its nest."

CHAPTER 8

NaCHO VaLLeY

Eddie buried what was left of the scrambled egg. The other eggs no longer purred. Instead, they made low, sad moaning sounds.

I knew this was important to Eddie, but it felt like we were wasting time. Finally I couldn't help myself. "Eddie, we have to go! Patty Anne's not my favorite person at the moment, but I can't abandon her to that thing!"

He had tears in his eyes. "We can't leave right now. It'll be dark any minute. You don't want to travel Lunch Lady Land at night."

"What do you mean, dark? It's been this bright out since I got here. It's not getting dark at all. We'll never catch the skybeater!"

Eddie shook his head. "You have to stop thinking like you're back in the world. This place is different. It doesn't slowly get dark. It's like someone hits the light switch."

Eddie huddled with the eggs, and a little while later, the fluorescent sun glowed dimly, then went black. I took one step and tripped over something. Nope, we weren't going to be able to find the skybeater until daylight.

As if reading my mind, Eddie said, "Look, I know where the skybeater is going. We don't need to track it. And I know you want to help your friend—"

"She's not really my friend," I said, feeling a little ashamed as the words came out of my mouth.

Eddie gave me a disapproving look. "Whatever's going on between you two, get over it. You need to work together, or you will literally not survive Lunch

Lady Land. What Patty Anne did was one of the bravest things I've ever seen. But it's a long, tough journey to the skybeater's nest and you look as exhausted as I feel. Let's get some rest and we'll head out at first light."

Eddie made sense, but it didn't help much. I lay on a makeshift marshmallow bed, my stomach in knots, my brain going a hundred miles an hour. This was all my fault. If I'd stopped Tim Connelly from putting gum on the chair, I wouldn't have gotten cafeteria duty, I wouldn't have found that stupid door, and Patty Anne wouldn't be clinging to the back of a monster flying through the dark. If anything happened to her .... One of the eggs pushed its way under my arm, purring. It helped. At some point, I drifted off to sleep. If I dreamed, I couldn't remember it.

"Josh, come on. Time to get moving." Eddie shook me awake. My head felt like it was full of instant mashed potatoes and I was sore all over. Lunch Lady was beating me up.

We had a quick breakfast of, what else, hotdog and french fries. "So now what? How do we find Patty Anne?" I asked.

"The skybeater has a nest on top of Neapolitan Mountain. But first we have to cross Nacho Valley."

"Ice cream and nachos? Sounds like a piece of cake!" Food analogies seemed to come naturally here.

"You have no idea. This won't be easy." Eddie strapped on a belt hung with dried-out grape skins as big as canteens. He handed me a belt too. "We'll stop for water on the way. Nacho Valley is like the Sahara, only hotter and drier."

I was starting to feel a little better. Yes, I was tired and still covered with old food, but my arms and legs no longer ached, my head was clear, and I knew what we had to accomplish. "I'm ready." Eddie gathered the eggs together and explained what we were doing.

"Do they understand what you're saying?" I asked.

"They seem to." The eggs squeezed around us in a big, round group hug. I was really starting to like the little guys.

We set off through the french fry meadow, following a wide path that Eddie and the eggs had beaten down. I wasn't even surprised when we reached a standard school water fountain standing all by itself in the field. The water was icy cold and delicious. I drank until my belly hurt. We filled the grape skins, and I cleaned myself up a bit. Now I was ready for anything.

The french fries ended abruptly at the top of a cliff. My heart dropped like an elevator with a snapped cable as I looked out over Nacho Valley. Jagged spikes and blades of nacho chips poked out of the ground at sharp angles. Crumbled chips covered the narrow spaces between them. I could see pools of hot cheese bubbling and smoking.

Eddie said, "Nice, huh? It's actually worse than it looks. The entire valley is a thin shell over a molten cheese lake. One wrong step and you're in the dip." He slapped my back. "So, it's a five-hour march if we move fast. You up for this?"

"Yeah. It's my fault Patty Anne's in trouble. Come on." We picked our way down the cliff. A spicy, burned-cheese smell assaulted my nostrils.

Eddie found a big nacho chip at the edge of the valley. He snapped it off at ground level. "Get yourself one of these. It makes a good shield."

"Shield against what?"

"Cheese geysers. They burst through narrow cracks, like little volcanoes. Burn like lava." Great. Cheese, my favorite food group, was now life-threatening.

Armed with our nacho chip shields, we started out. Not bad at first. The broken chips shifted underfoot, but I quickly learned to watch where I walked. I tried not to impale myself as my clothes snagged on sharp chip edges. Heat radiated up from the ground in visible waves. It was Death Valley hot. Center of the earth hot.

I was sweating like a boiled hotdog after a couple of minutes, and I smelled like picnic food left out in the sun too long. It felt like sweat was running out of my pores faster than I could drink.

We were circling around an especially large cheese pool when I heard a loud, wet hissing sound. Eddie yelled, "Duck and cover!" I looked at him with a blank expression. "Like this!" He dropped to the ground and pulled the nacho shield over him. I did the same.

Just in time! A geyser erupted right between us, spewing hot nacho cheese everywhere. It battered my shield while I huddled underneath. Big gobs hit the ground, hissing and smoking. Then it was over, just like that. Eddie said, "Stay where you are for a minute. Give the cheese a chance to cool." Fine by me. My nostrils burned from the spicy eruption.

We picked up our speed when we got going again. My shield was heavier with its rubbery coating of cheese, and I was really dragging. I started to peel it off, but Eddie said, "Hey, don't do that. It'll come in handy later." I was too tired to argue.

The next few hours were more of the same. We had to duck and cover twice, and once my foot broke through a weak spot in the ground. I had a quick glimpse of the underground cheese lake before Eddie grabbed my shirt and yanked me to safety. Nacho Valley stunk, big time.

I began to make out the cliff line at the edge of the valley. Finally. When we were fifty yards away, I thought, *We're home free.* Famous last words. The ground beneath us lurched to one side, throwing us both down. It started to shake. Pieces of chips shattered and flew through the air. "Eddie!" I yelled, "now what?"

"Oh no, this isn't good. Josh, put your shield on the ground, cheese side down, and climb on."

"Then what?" I tried to keep my voice from sounding too hysterical.

"Hang on!"

A geyser the size of Old Faithful erupted right beneath us. We were thrown into the air on a huge wave of cheese, bouncing up and down, spinning wildly. I clung to my nacho chip wakeboard, squeezed my eyes shut, and waited to die.

I felt myself lift even higher, and then I was upside-down, free falling. I don't care what they say; my life did not pass before my eyes. I was too busy screaming to watch a mental movie. I opened my eyes for a millisecond, and saw nacho knife blades surrounded by boiling cheese death headed straight for me.

CHAPTER 9

Ice cream, you scream

I landed headfirst in something freezing cold. I dug myself out, happy to be alive. The nacho cheese tsunami had thrown me clear over the cliff and onto the foothills of Neapolitan Mountain. There I was, waist deep in strawberry ice cream. All things considered, it could have been worse.

"Josh! You okay?" Eddie trudged toward me across the surface on some kind of snowshoes. He carried my nacho chip shield on his back.

"Yeah, I'm fine. A little shook up is all."

"Here. You're going to need this." He broke my shield roughly in half. "Climb up on these and squish your feet into the cheese. Takes some getting used to, but it's the only way to walk on top of the ice cream."

I got my chip snowshoes on and took a couple of shaky steps. Weird, but not bad. Like walking on water with inner tubes strapped to your feet. "All right. Point me toward the next dangerous situation."

Eddie laughed. "Josh, you're a funny guy."

"Some people would say stupid."

"Yeah, well, I hope some people would say lucky too. We're going to need it where we're going." He pointed straight up. Neapolitan Mountain towered above us: first strawberry, then vanilla, then chocolate. Swirling clouds of mist hid the top of the mountain.

"Let me guess. Killer ice cream scoopers. Deadly hot fudge rivers."

"Nah, but you're close. Just cross your fingers we don't run into trouble. Let's climb."

Climb we did, for what seemed like forever. The rough bottoms of the chips were great for traction, but it was still tough going. Plus it was cold enough for my breath to puff out in little clouds.

We inched our way around a frozen pink outcropping and there, straight ahead, was the strawberry-vanilla dividing line. Only one problem. Between where we stood and the first vanilla plateau was a deep chasm. A crazy jumble of tall, narrow towers of ice cream soared up from the icy depths. They swayed a little in the sharp breeze. The other side of the chasm looked like it was a football field away. I bent over to catch my breath and looked sideways at Eddie.

"Please tell me there's a nice bridge across this somewhere," I said.

Eddie laughed and shook his head. "A bridge would be helpful, but no, afraid not. Those towers are more stable than they look. The idea is you jump from one to the next, all the way across."

"Seriously?" From what I could see, they were scattered around at least six feet apart and not much more than three feet across at best.

"It's not so bad once you get the hang of it."

"It's the getting the hang of it part that worries me," I said. "Okay, let's do this."

Eddie clapped his hands together. "All right! Whatever you do, keep your balance and make sure you land on your snowshoes. Otherwise you could slide right off. Watch me." Eddie perched on the edge, lined up with the nearest tower. He bent his knees, swung his arms a couple of times, and launched himself into the air. Eddie stuck his landing with just a little wobble, his snowshoes squarely on target. He glanced back and said, "Just follow me." Then he faced the next tower and jumped.

I cautiously crept up to the edge and peeked over. I couldn't see the bottom. I bent my knees a couple of times and gave my arms an experimental swing. When I looked up, Eddie was several jumps ahead.

"Come on, Josh!" he yelled.

I leaped. The ice cream tower looked like it was about a mile away. I hadn't jumped far enough! I looked down into dark, bottomless death, but then my snowshoes hit ice cream with a solid thunk. My body pitched forward, and I landed on my hands and knees. I totally did not stick my landing, but I was still alive, so I gave myself style points for that.

Eddie was now more than halfway across the chasm. I followed, leapfrogging from one tower to the next. My landings got better, but my legs were turning to rubber and my jumps were coming up shorter and shorter. When Eddie reached the other side, he cheered me on.

Two towers from the end, I slipped on takeoff. I pinwheeled my arms, trying to stay upright as I sailed through the air. My right foot landed where it should have, but the left bounced off the tower side, missing completely, and I did the splits. I should probably mention here that the splits is not something I do regularly. I threw my body forward, dug my hands in and managed to pull myself up.

"Josh, don't do that!" Eddie screamed. "You just about gave me a heart attack."

I climbed shakily to my feet. "Got it," I said. "Sorry. I'll try not to give you a heart attack." I made the last leap and collapsed in a heap. I said, "Eddie, please, I gotta rest for a minute."

Eddie plopped down right where he was. "Yeah, I could use a break myself."

When I was breathing normally again, I said, "Wow, that was crazy. Except for the whole possibility of dying thing, it was almost fun. Like a really tricky video game level."

Eddie looked puzzled. "Video game?" he said. "You mean, like Pong? That was nothing like Pong."

I slapped Eddie on the back and said, "My friend, you have no idea what you've missed back in the real world." *I just hope I get a chance to play video games again*, I thought.

Eddie scooped up some ice cream and took a big bite. "Oh well. Good old Lunch Lady Land. The food's great as long as you can manage to stay alive."

I tried a taste. "Not bad, but I don't really like vanilla." I made a mental note to try the chocolate.

The vanilla zone climb was tougher. Our path got steeper, winding between unstable crags and around deep crevasses. There were football-sized peanuts scattered all over the place that broke loose underfoot. I can't count the number of times I went down. Luckily, my face kept breaking my fall. The wind had picked up, and my hands were burning from the cold. One more reason not to like vanilla.

We were inching sideways along a narrow ridge when a big glop of ice cream smacked me right on the nose. Another dropped squarely on top of my head. Then the sky opened up.

Heavy scoops of ice cream pelted us. I could barely see Eddie through the thick blizzard. "Keep moving!" he yelled. "These storms don't usually last long. But if you stand still, you'll be buried!"

I put my head down and forged ahead, half-blinded. I tried my best not to get knocked off the mountain, or buried under it. Once, a wind gust caught me. I spun around, slipped on a peanut, and my foot came down on nothing but air. I hopped away on the other foot, wheeled my arms, and managed to get back on firm ice cream.

The blizzard ended gradually. By the time we reached the chocolate level of Neapolitan Mountain, it was down to the occasional wet splat. We crested the next rise and stopped to shovel out our snowshoes and wipe some of the gunk off. Eddie looked like the Abominable Snowman having a bad hair day. I'm sure I looked just as bad.

Stretched out before us was a wide, gently rising slope that led to the final peak. The top was still hidden behind a curtain of clouds. *This doesn't look so bad*, I thought. Of course, every time I thought that it got me in trouble.

Eddie shaded his eyes and slowly scanned back and forth. "Looks clear."

"What are we looking for?"

"Spoonies."

"I'm a glutton for punishment, so I'll bite. What's a spoonie?"

Eddie never took his eyes off the frosty chocolate. "You know those little wooden spoons you get with cups of ice cream? Spoonies look like those. Except six feet long and mean as all getout. They corkscrew through this big field of ice cream like spinning sharks, burrowing tunnels wherever they go. Spoonies sense vibrations like a shark smells blood. They feel you on the surface, dig up underneath and drop you into the tunnels. So they can feed."

"Given the choice, I would prefer not to be food. We can't go around?"

"Nope. It's a sheer drop on all sides."

"I'm adding ice cream to the list of things I'm going to give up if I ever get back home."

70

"Yeah, that's what I said about hotdogs. You get over it." Eddie shook his arms and legs, like a runner loosening up before a race. "Listen, the trick is to stick as close as you can to the rim of the bowl, and try to move smoothly. Kind of like cross country skiing." Sadly, I've never skied.

We dropped into the bowl. The skiing thing wasn't working for me, but I tried to place my feet as quietly as possible. We headed to the right. Halfway around I was moving pretty good. That's when the first spoonie appeared.

"Josh," Eddie said quietly. "Look out in the middle there." A big wooden fin surfaced, then slid back into the ice cream. It was heading in our direction. *Great*, I thought, *here comes Jaws.*

CHAPTER 10

WHO'S RESCUING WHO?

It surfaced again, much closer. And it had friends. "I think they're onto us!" I said.

"Forget about being smooth. Run!"

Easier said than done. Nacho chip snowshoes are not made for running. I staggered along like a two-year-old wearing his dad's shoes. Half a dozen spoonies jumped clear out of the ice cream less than ten feet away, spinning wildly, close enough to splash us on reentry. They were relatively thin, but had ridiculously big V-shaped mouths lined with chainsaw teeth that continually whirred and ripped down the beasts' gullets. These things weren't like sharks at all. They made sharks look like guppies.

"We're not going to make it!" I screamed.

Eddie's left foot sank. He started to tip. I hooked my elbow under his arm and heaved. It would have been a perfect rescue, except I heaved a little too hard. We bounced, tangled together, then slid toward the edge. And over.

We jerked to a stop side by side, fingers dug into the rim of a smooth, frozen wall of ice cream. Our feet dangled above a crevasse in the mountain so deep that just looking made me dizzy.

"Thanks, Josh." Eddie managed to sound sincere while hanging over a yawning chasm.

"You're welcome, but it could have ended better."

"Even so. Unfortunately, I have some more bad news. Listen."

It took me a minute to hear it—that familiar shrieking metal on metal sound. The skybeater.

I tried to kick my feet up and over the edge, but

it just wasn't happening. When Eddie and I tried to work together, we almost knocked each other off the wall. We hung there and waited for the skybeater to come and scramble us. I was too exhausted, and too scared, to even talk.

The slashing metal beater sound got louder. The air around me vibrated, and the mountain seemed to shake with the noise. I felt my skin try to crawl right off my body as a dark shadow passed over us. A tornado of wind sucked me away from the ice cream wall, then jammed me back against it. I lost my grip and swung one-handed for a second before I managed to grab hold again.

The skybeater circled around and came in below us. I didn't want to see the carnage, so I closed my eyes. Then I heard Patty Anne's voice say, "Hey guys, need a lift?"

Peachy, I thought, *I'm hearing things.* Maybe that's what happens when you're about to die.

Eddie must have looked down, because he

whooped and hollered like he had just won the lottery. I chanced a peek. Patty Anne rode the sky-beater like it was a Shetland pony at the county fair. I laughed, a little hysterically.

"Boy am I glad to see you!" I shouted.

"You and me both!" said Eddie. "But what—?"

"Let's save explanations for later and get you off that cliff first. I'm going to come up under the two of you as close as I can, but she's not so good at hovering. Then you can drop down on the skybeater's back." She patted the side of the beast and said, "Okay, Skybaby, nice and easy. Go get my friends." She called it Skybaby. Crazy.

The skybeater flew straight up, closing the gap between us. Just as it got near enough for us to drop, the beater closest to the wall swung in too far and hit. A fountain of ice cream sprayed over us. Patty Anne hung on as the skybeater shook from the shock, trying to regain control. "Jump, guys! I can't hold it here much longer."

I steadied myself and looked over at Eddie. "Ready?"

"Ready."

The skybeater hovered just below us. I silently counted to three and pushed off from the wall.

Then the lights went out.

I couldn't see a thing. I heard Eddie land with a thud on the skybeater's back, and I spread out my arms to cushion my landing. Instead I just kept falling. It felt like I fell for about three days. I thought about stuff, like how much my mom and dad were going to miss me. I thought about my little brother, Topher. He could be a pain in the rear end, but I really liked having a little brother. I thought about Patty Anne. Two days ago, I thought she was the Queen of All Dorks. Now I thought she was the bravest, smartest person I had ever met. She had somehow tamed a monster and tried to rescue me, except that I had botched a perfectly good rescue. I thought about Eddie Eggs and his round, purring buddies.

I kept falling. I wondered if I would feel anything when I landed. I hoped it wouldn't hurt too much.

I heard a roaring in my ears. At first I thought it was the wind blowing by me, but it got louder, and I strained to see. The darkness was total. *Hearing things again*, I thought.

I hit bottom.

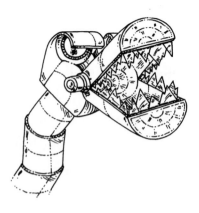

CHAPTER 11

CANISAUR

Heaven was a bed as warm as the summer sun and soft as a cloud. It was perfect, except for the bees. They wouldn't stop buzzing in my ears. I shooed them away and tried to cover my head, but they kept right on buzzing. Pretty darn annoying for heaven.

Then the bees started talking. "Josh. Wake up, Josh." They even knew my name. How weird. "Josh!" Wait a minute. I knew that voice.

I forced my eyes open, like prying up a manhole cover with a crowbar. It wasn't worth the effort. Either I was blind, or it was as dark as the inside of a spoonie's belly. Spoonies? It all came back to me then. Lunch Lady Land, Neapolitan Mountain, the skybeater …. "Hey! I'm not dead! This isn't heaven."

"You're awake!" Patty Anne yelled, which made my head hurt, but that was okay. She hugged me and that was okay too. Weird, but okay. Maybe we were done being dueling jerks.

"Yeah, I guess I am." I tried to sit up and fell over sideways. My stomach did a somersault.

"Welcome back, partner," Eddie said. He propped me back up.

"Where am I? Why am I alive? I hit bottom."

Patty Anne laughed. "You didn't hit bottom; you hit the skybeater's back. We swooped down and caught you."

"That's impossible. It was pitch black!"

"Didn't you know? My skybaby can see in the dark."

I was still dizzy, but my head was clearing. "You have a pet name for this killer. And you hugged me. How long was I out?"

"Hours," Eddie said. "We were really worried. We took turns sleeping so one of us could keep an eye on you."

"Patty Anne, what's with the skybaby stuff? Did you actually make friends with that monster?"

"She's not a monster. And don't forget she saved your life." I could tell from the stern, serious tone in Patty Anne's voice that she felt strongly about this. "She can't help acting like she does. She was created to be a challenge for the lunch ladies. She's programmed to attack stuff."

"And you know all this because …"

"She told me. In my head, with pictures. At first she tried to throw me off, but no way I was letting go. Once I calmed down, she starting talking to me. Telepathically, I guess you could call it. She's the only creature in this whole place with the ability to communicate mind to mind. The lunch ladies wanted her to be a formidable foe, but she's even smarter than they planned. And I can talk back to her the same way! She's a completely reformed mean machine."

It sounded as nutso as everything else in Lunch Lady Land, but I trusted Patty Anne. Still, it seemed like a big pill for Eddie to swallow. "Eddie, are you cool with this?"

"Absolutely. I talked to her too. No more scrambled eggs."

As Eddie said "eggs," the lights clicked on. I yelped before I could stop myself. My heavenly bed was the skybeater's nest. It was a thick mound of shredded vegetables as big around as a swimming pool, perched on the highest peak of Neapolitan Mountain. The skybeater sprawled in her nest, watching us calmly. She had been there the whole time.

"This nice skybeater business is going to take some getting used to," I said.

Oh boy. I got this strange feeling, like fingers

poking around in my head, but it didn't hurt. Then I saw a series of pictures that my brain translated as, "Good morning, Josh. I'm glad you're okay."

I tried to send back, "Thanks," but I don't know if she got it.

Eddie stood up. "Okay, kids, time to get you to the lunch ladies. With skybaby here giving us a lift, it won't take nearly as long as walking." That was fine by me. I felt like one big bruise.

We climbed aboard. Patty Anne scratched the skybeater between the eyes. I could tell they were chatting. She looked back at us. "Hang on, guys. Here we go. And, um, Josh, about that hug. What with all this saving each other, holding a grudge seems a little silly."

"Works for me," I said.

The skybeater revved her rotors and shot off the nest. As clanky as she sounded, the ride was surprisingly smooth. I settled back to enjoy the view, but there wasn't much to see yet. Clouds wrapped around the top of the mountain like cotton candy.

The cloud cover thinned, then disappeared. Lunch Lady Land spread out below us.

"Oh ... my ... goodness," Patty Anne stammered.

My thought exactly. If Dr. Seuss had been obsessed with food, and painted landscapes, they might have looked like Lunch Lady Land.

Leaving Neapolitan Mountain behind, we flew over a massive cauliflower and broccoli forest. Two rivers, one white milk and one chocolate, twisted through the vegetable trees. They met where the forest ended, at the top of a canyon. The rivers tumbled over the edge in a waterfall bigger than Niagara, mixing together, forming a wide, slow waterway that split the canyon floor.

"Eddie," I said, "is that canyon what I think it is?"

"Chocolate. Miles and miles of chocolate. I guess even the lunch ladies need a treat now and then."

We followed the path of the chocolate canyon for a little while, then changed direction. The skybeater cruised over one wonder after another. I saw white bread sailboats tacking lazily on the surface of a chili mac lake. There were fish sticks stacked at crazy angles hundreds of feet high, like desert rock formations. Hush-puppy boulders balanced on top.

Chocolate chip cookie plateaus, vanilla wafer islands bobbing in a sea of banana pudding .... Lunch Lady Land was pretty cool if you were flying above it and nothing was trying to kill you. Up high like this, the smell was downright pleasant. Just faint traces, like walking through a grocery store deli.

"Almost there, guys," Eddie said. "Cafeteria Castle, where the lunch ladies live, is on the other side of the Great Lasagna Swamp. You're going to love this. Just be glad we don't have to cross it on foot."

We flew over the swamp. Bubbling hot mozzarella, spitting pools of red sauce: it made Nacho Valley look like Disneyland. Small garlic bread islands dotted the swamp. Groves of breadstick trees sprouted from each island, but it was hard to see them because the islands were half buried in steaming mounds of something green and gooey. Creatures shambled through the lasagna. They looked prehistoric, like dinosaurs bolted together from huge tin cans. The creatures moved slowly, long metal tails swinging back and forth, long metal necks foraging for whatever it was they ate. Kids who didn't belong there, probably.

"I call them canisaurs," Eddie said.

They were seriously cool dinos. "Hey, can we swoop down for a closer look?" I asked. "How about it, Skybeater?" I guess she heard me, because she banked and dropped into a long circular glide, ending in a hover just above the closest canisaur.

Patty Anne said, "Josh, we don't have time for sightseeing. I want to go home."

"Oh, come on, I'm a red-blooded American boy, which means I love dinosaurs. Even weird ones constructed from jumbo food storage containers. Please?"

Patty Anne shot me a look that could have curdled milk.

"Okay, okay," I said. "But you gotta admit, that is one impressive ... whatever it is." Up close it was more than impressive—it was terrifying. Enormous rusted metal cylinders held together with bolts the size of Volkswagen Bugs. Its hinged mouth was like a two-car garage lined with ragged scrap metal teeth. Hooded searchlight eyes scanned the swamp, searching for prey. Each lumbering step unleashed a geyser of hot sauce and shredded pasta. The canisaurs called to each other across the swamp, bellowing like broken foghorns. Reluctantly I said, "Okay, Skybeater, let's get to that castle."

The canisaur had other ideas. As Skybeater spun in the direction of the castle, the canisaur's head snapped up with surprising speed. It laser-focused on us, and its searchlight eyes briefly blinded me.

"Get us out of here, Skybaby!" Patty Anne yelled. The rotors wound up another notch and we shot forward—right into the path of the canisaur's massive spiked tail. It whipped through the air, spraying sauce and blotting out the sun. The three of us lurched in different directions, trying to duck, but there was nowhere to go. The tail slammed into us like a runaway freight train, with a crash of metal on metal louder than anything I had ever heard.

What happened next felt like slow motion. Skybeater was knocked clean out from under us, flipping end over beaters, motor roaring. I was flung high into the sky, my body flopping around like a ragdoll. I caught a glimpse of Patty Anne above me, and Eddie just below. Then we hit the top of our arc and gravity remembered to kick in. We tumbled back toward hot, bubbling death about a mile below. I decided to spend the rest of my too-short life screaming. It seemed reasonable. By the sound of it, Patty Anne and Eddie had the same idea. Luckily something appeared to break our fall. The gaping, jagged mouth of the canisaur.

CHAPTER 12

IN THE BELLY
OF THE BEAST

It looked like we were hurtling into a vertical cave mouth. I twisted my body like I was doing yoga as I tried to avoid the serrated edges of the monster's teeth while its mouth closed around us. One tooth snagged my shirt and tore through it like it was toilet paper. On the plus side, it could have been my face, so lucky me.

The jaws closed tightly, plunging us into darkness.

Then I bounced down the canisaur's long throat. Every couple of yards was a ridge where the neck flexed, and I hit every one on the way down. Patty Anne and Eddie did the same. Occasionally we took a break from bouncing off hard metal ridges and bounced off each other instead. This seemed to go on for about three weeks.

"Hey!" I heard Eddie yell, "I think I see—oof!—a light—ow!—down there!" He was right. When I managed to land facing the right direction, there was definitely a faint glow.

The throat leveled out and I rolled to a stop, wedged upside down against a slab of metal. I wondered how the others were doing, then got my answer a second later when Eddie landed on my head with a splat, followed by Patty Anne. Ouch and double ouch.

We untangled ourselves, checking to make sure we hadn't lost any important bits on the way down. By now it was bright enough to see each other in the murky green light. I felt bruised and battered, but nothing appeared to be broken. Patty Anne and Eddie groaned as they touched tender spots.

"That went well," I said and tried to laugh, but it made my ribs hurt. "I'm adding slides to the list of things I'm never doing again if we get out of this."

"It could have been worse. At least we're alive," Patty Anne said.

"Give it time," I said. "The day's still young."

Eddie smiled and said, "Do either of you happen to have a Lunch Lady Land-sized can opener?"

"Hey, guys," Patty Anne said. "What is that horrible smell?" Her face looked like it was turning inside out. I was so worried about bodily harm that I hadn't noticed it. Now it hit me, a nasty, foul scent. I once forgot a stringer of catfish in a cooler in the back of my dad's minivan. For a week. By the time we found it, the inside of his car smelled like a fish market that ran out of ice during a heat wave. This was like that, mixed with spoiled cabbage and rotten cheese, the kind that smells like armpits even when it's fresh.

"I'm almost afraid to find out, but let's have a look," I said. We had landed in a small depression at the base of the canisaur's throat. The three of us crawled slowly up to the lip and looked into the belly of the beast, where the glow, and the smell, came from. "Seriously?" I said.

"What the—?" Eddie said.

"This is messed up," Patty Anne said, and I had to agree. The inside of the canisaur was one vast, hollow space crisscrossed with corroded metal girders, broken pipes, and random hunks of sheet metal. Stringy globs of slime hung like Spanish moss from every surface. But that wasn't the messed up part. The beast's belly was filled with the decomposing remains of whatever it ate, an ocean of moldy cheese, rancid sauce and big, unrecognizable lumps that must have once been Lunch Lady Land creatures.

Cruising through the toxic soup like nightmarish motorboats were hundreds of fat, round monsters the size of beach balls. They were covered in boils that pulsed and crawled beneath their skin. Their enormous mouths sucked in everything in their paths, crunching away with obvious glee. Huge jets of sludge spurted out behind them. The monsters were the source of the light we had seen; they glowed a sickly vomit green.

"Any guesses what those things are?" I asked. I tried to talk without breathing, which doesn't work all that well, but my gag reflex was on high alert.

"I think they're bacteria," Patty Anne said. "They help the canisaur digest its food."

"Okay, that's gross," I said. "And yet strangely cool."

Patty Anne and Eddie looked at me like my head had spun completely around. "Fine, not cool. Not cool at all. Moving on, how do we avoid getting digested by giant mutant bacteria and escape?"

Eddie had been pretty quiet, his brow furrowed like he was working something out. "I have two thoughts," he said. "And you're not going to like either of them. I don't like them. First, all that twisted metal up there"—he pointed to the scrap that lined the inside of the canisaur—"we may be able to climb our way through it to the other end of this walking tin can." I looked up and got dizzy. Great, I thought, now I'm going to have to add monkey bars to the list of things I'm giving up.

Patty Anne looked a little green, and I don't think it was just from the light of the bacteria. "What's the other thing, Eddie?" she asked.

"We came in the same way everything else in here did. Maybe we can leave the same way everything else does."

"Hold it," I said. "Are you saying ...? What are you saying?"

Patty Anne smiled, just a little, and said, "I think Eddie is suggesting that canisaurs poop just like everybody else. And that's how we can escape."

"Boy, Lunch Lady Land just gets better and better," I said. "So we're going out the back door."

"That's pretty much it," Eddie said. "I'm open to any other ideas. I'm kind of hoping one of you has one, because I think this one stinks—literally."

We sat in glum silence for a minute. "Nope, nothing," I said.

"Me neither," Patty Anne said.

"Right," Eddie said. "Let's do it."

Famous last words, I thought.

It wasn't bad, at least at first. It was just like climbing through a rusty, broken-down jungle gym on an abandoned, overgrown playground. With schools of glowing, carnivorous beach balls swimming in the toxic soup far below. So, not totally like a jungle gym, but sort of similar. The ribbons of slime hanging from the bars were dangerously slippery, and I had to place each hand and foot with care. I was still making good time, and Eddie was even faster than me. Patty Anne was a whole different story. She swung through the metal maze like one of those forkmonkeys. I was no longer mad at her, but I had to admit it was kind of annoying. I kept waiting for her to screech.

"Hey, Patty Anne," I called. "Have you done this before?"

She looked back at me, and a shadow passed over her face. She said, "When you get picked on during recess, you need an escape route. The monkey bars were mine. Turns out bullies give up easily. And some of them are scared of heights." Yet one more reason for me to feel bad for past behavior. I had never bullied anyone, but I hadn't stopped it either. Lunch Lady Land was like one of those movies my mom watched on Lifetime. Always teaching you lessons.

Patty Anne stopped suddenly. When I reached her and Eddie, I found out why. We were facing a long gap in the structure, much too far to jump. The break ran as far as I could see to the left and right in the dim light. We were stuck.

"No way!" I said with more confidence than I felt. "We are not going back and I am not dying inside a smelly tin can!" I looked around in desperate search of an idea. My eyes landed on a crossbar at least twenty feet long. I gave it a good shake, and the far end rattled loosely. A good sign. The near end was screwed into a corroded hub that did not look promising.

Lefty loosey, righty tighty, I thought, and gave a twist. Nothing. I put some weight behind it, and it budged, just a little.

Patty Anne scooped up a handful of belly slime. She said, "Here, try greasing it up with this."

"Why not," I said. I rubbed it around the pipe threads, working it in as far as I could. "Here goes nothing. Eddie, lend me a hand." We both wrapped our hands around the pipe and twisted. It gave, with a nails-on-a-blackboard squeak. After several turns that got progressively easier, the end popped out. Eddie and I rearranged ourselves for a better grip, gave the pole a solid yank, and the far end snapped off. So far, so good.

Patty Anne joined us, and we fed the pole out

into the gap until it dropped with a bouncing clang on the far structure. I found a good spot to rest it on our end, and we had a little bridge. "Patty Anne, you're the lightest," I said. "How do you feel about going first? Then we'll have someone holding on at either end." She didn't give it a second thought, just reached up and took hold of the pole. Patty Anne scooted down the pole hand over hand. It jumped a little but held, and she was safe in the structure on the other side in seconds. Patty Anne held the other end down tight.

"Okay, Eddie, you next," I said. He started to argue, but I shook my head. "My crazy idea, so I go last." Eddie grabbed on and stepped off. The pole sagged a little, but Eddie crossed without a hitch. "Right, my turn," I said. I reset my end of the pole and gave it a good tug to test it out. Patty Anne and Eddie wrapped their arms around their end and braced themselves. "Be there in a sec," I said.

I took hold of the pole, dropped my legs out into

space—and my end came free with a sickening lurch. The pole swung like a pendulum, me clinging on white-knuckled.

"Hold on!" I screamed. I caught a glimpse of Eddie and Patty Anne frantically trying to trap the pole between them as I rocked back the other way, and then I was vertical, hands wrapped around the pole end, feet dangling helplessly.

I heard a splash, followed by several more, and looked down. Wouldn't you know it? The little green monsters could *jump*!

CHAPTER 13

DOWN THE DRAIN

Have you ever been at the zoo during feeding time? The zookeepers walk from cage to cage with buckets full of dead stuff, tossing handfuls to ravenous animals who jump and snap for the yummiest tidbits. At that exact moment, I felt like the yummiest tidbit of all. The little beast balls propelled themselves out of the sewage on jets of goop, jaws snapping for my feet. Too low at first, they sailed a little higher with every leap. I chanced a look up.

Patty Anne and Eddie were struggling just to hang on to their end.

"I'm climbing up! Don't let go!" I yelled, trying to be encouraging.

I let go with my left hand and grabbed on higher, then did the same with the right. I was about to go again when I felt something bump my foot. One of the green meanies! The next one came at me, mouth like a garbage can lined with teeth, and I kicked it right in the nose. It shrieked and tumbled back, taking three of its friends with it. That was my chance. I scurried up the pole, muscles straining. Once I could wrap my legs around the pole, it got a little easier, like climbing the rope in gym class.

Patty Anne and Eddie were just a few feet above me, and I thought I was home free. Then my hand hit a slimy patch on the pole and I started to slide. I caught myself halfway down and began to climb again, being extra careful. The bacteria had stopped jumping and were now circling beneath me like buzzards circling a hurt animal.

Hopefully they don't know something I don't, I thought. Then hands hauled me up to safety.

I gave Patty Anne and Eddie a quick hug. "Let's get out of here," I said. "I no longer think this dino is in any way cool."

"I felt like we were fishing and you were bait," Patty Anne said.

"Well, I'm glad you didn't catch anything," I said.

Eddie laughed. "You two are kind of funny together," he said. "Like a comedy team."

"I'll take that as a compliment," I said.

"Me too," Patty Anne said. "Let's climb."

Back into the bizarro monkey bars. We swung, crawled, slid, climbed, wiggled, and wormed our way through the canisaur scaffolding, toward the back of the beast. We arrived in a tangle of bars just above the huge opening that led to the canisaur's mammoth hollow tail. "Okay," Eddie said. "Watch that area below the tail. We should know soon enough if I'm right."

Nothing happened. The minutes stretched for what seemed like hours. I said, "Eddie, what are we watching for? Whatever it is, it's not—"

"Wait, I think something's happening," Patty Anne said.

She was right. The green monsters seemed agitated. They bumped into each other in their haste to clear the immediate area. The thick, digested swill began to move in a circular motion. It swirled, faster and faster, like a whirlpool, big goopy chunks bobbing along. Right in the center of the whirlpool, an opening appeared. Liquid thundered through in a smelly flood. Seconds later the opening slammed shut. The monsters quickly returned to their digestive duties.

Patty Anne said, "You were right, Eddie. Not that I'm really looking forward to this."

Something had been nagging at me, and I finally realized what it was. "Question," I said. "How do we know we won't drop through this thing's rear end and land right in a boiling hot pool of sauce and cheese? I don't want to end up another lasagna layer."

"Didn't I tell you?" Eddie said. "Canisaurs only poop on the garlic bread islands. That's what all the slime you saw was. They use them like giant litter boxes."

"I guess that's comforting, sort of," I said.

"And disgusting, sort of," Patty Anne added. "Hey, check it out," she said, pointing down.

The bacteria were moving away. The goop began to swirl. "This is it," I said. "Get ready." We centered ourselves over the middle of the whirlpool at least twenty feet below.

"That's a long drop," Patty Anne said, a hint of worry in her voice.

"Don't worry," I said. "All that poop will break your fall."

Patty Anne punched me lightly in the shoulder. "You always know just what to say to a girl," she said.

The floodgates opened. We held hands.

"One—" I said.

"Two—" Patty Anne said.

"Three!" Eddie yelled, and we jumped.

Our aim was true. We hit the sludge and immediately got yanked apart, caught in the swirling vortex. Then I was falling, caught in a thick wet blanket of crud. It filled my mouth and nose, covered my eyes, enveloped my body. I bounced on a spongy surface, choking, coughing up goop, and gasping for air. I rolled to a stop and jumped to my feet, trying to wipe my face and shake everything off my body.

Patty Anne and Eddie had landed near me. I could see them dancing the same jig I had in a futile attempt to get clean.

"It worked. We're alive!" Eddie said.

"And covered in poop," Patty Anne said. "I thought I was dirty before." She stood like a scarecrow, arms out at her sides. She looked miserable.

"Aw, come on," I said. "It's not so bad." I found a clean piece of garlic bread turf, broke off a buttery chunk, and popped it in my mouth. "Not bad," I said. "For a litter box."

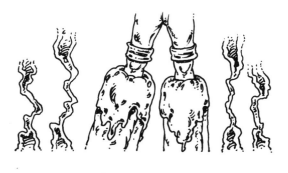

CHAPTER 14

THE GREAT LASAGNA SWAMP

First things first, we had to clean up at least a little. Patty Anne had the great idea to use big hunks of garlic bread as sponges. It was dense and absorbent enough to do the job, and we managed to remove a couple layers of nastiness. Patty Anne was still making disgusted faces, but at least we were no longer giving off waves of stink. Once you got away from the dino waste, the lasagna actually smelled good.

I said, "So Eddie, lay it out for us. Where do we stand?"

"Let's see. We were about halfway across the swamp before we were so rudely interrupted. So we still have a couple of miles to go while avoiding the canisaurs and the boiling hot sauce and cheese."

"That's all?" I said, with as much sarcasm as I could manage.

"And then we arrive at Cafeteria Castle?" Patty Anne asked.

"Well, no," Eddie said. "But let's worry about one thing at a time."

Uh-oh. I had the feeling there was something important he wasn't telling us, but I let it pass. "So how do we get out of this mess?" I said.

"I don't have an answer for this one," Eddie said. "I've done my best to avoid the Great Lasagna Swamp. I don't even like lasagna. I'm more of a ravioli guy myself."

"I'm sure there's a man-eating ravioli around here

somewhere," I said.

Eddie laughed and said, "Not so far, but you never know."

Patty Anne kept looking at the breadstick trees in the center of the island. "Eddie, how deep is the swamp?" she asked.

"Not very," he said. "Maybe five, six feet."

"Huh," she said. "I'm just thinking out loud here, so work with me. Last summer I volunteered at the Serling Heights Charity Carnival."

Of course you did, I almost said, then stopped myself. A cheap shot that she didn't deserve.

"I learned how to walk on stilts as part of the show. It's surprisingly easy. Those oversized breadsticks there—I think they'd work as stilts."

"So we're going to walk across the swamp?" I said.

My face must have betrayed my thoughts, because Patty Anne crossed her arms and said, "Hey! Don't knock it until you try it."

Eddie was more diplomatic. "It ... could ... work."

Not really a ringing endorsement.

Patty Anne threw up her hands at our obvious lack of vision and said, "Fine, I'll show you!" and stomped off. She found a stand of trees the canisaurs had managed not to splash. Patty Anne picked one and shimmied right up. The girl could really climb. She perched on top of her chosen breadstick tree, pointed one toe, and dug her foot into the knee. "Here's the tricky part," she said as she reached her other foot across to a nearby treetop, pulled it toward her, and dug that foot in as well.

Patty Anne towered over us wearing her giant bread stilts, hands on her hips, a big smile on her face. "Here's the other tricky part," she said. She twisted her legs back and forth until the two breadstick trees snapped off at the surface with a satisfying crunch. Patty Anne took a couple of tentative steps. "Not bad!" she said, and strode off. She circled the island with big, crusty steps. "Come on, guys, give it a try!"

Eddie and I looked at each other and shrugged,

then set off to find our own trees. I could tell you that I had run right up one of those breadsticks, planted both feet, given a quick wiggle and started to tap dance, but that would be a lie. It took me forever just to climb to the top, and I nearly fell off half a dozen times. I managed the first foot, but getting the second one attached was not pretty. Doing the splits was starting to be a habit.

By the sound of it, Eddie had similar difficulties. Patty Anne shouted out helpful suggestions between fits of giggles, then kept right on laughing as we finally broke free and staggered around getting used to our new legs. It turned out Patty Anne was right. After a bit of shuffling, I got the hang of it.

"It's actually kind of fun!" I said. I stepped with more confidence.

"This will actually work! Nice job, Patty Anne," Eddie said as he walked around, getting steadier with each step.

"Thank you, Eddie," said Patty Anne. "Now if you

two are done playing around, can we hit the swamp?"

We hit the swamp. Between the pasta sheets floating in sauce and the layers of melted mozzarella, you couldn't take big steps. It was more of a sliding motion, pushing through the gooey mess. The smell was downright intoxicating. It feels sacrilegious to say, but my nose was even happier than when I visited Rudy Bennaducci's house. Sorry, Grandma Bennaducci.

It turned out the canisaurs weren't a problem. They were so big and so noisy, splashing around and bellowing to each other, that they were easy to avoid. We were only a couple of feet above the swamp surface, so we kept a low profile. When possible we kept garlic bread islands between them and us. Those mountains of crud helped hide us.

My biggest issue was the heat. It didn't seem to bother Patty Anne and Eddie, but I was dying. I felt like I was skating across a sizzling griddle. Sweat literally popped off my skin, like grease off a sausage link. My own ripeness was distracting from the heavenly lasagna scent. Really annoying. "Hey, why aren't you guys sweating as much as me? I'm melting like this mozzarella!" I complained.

"Is it hot? I hadn't noticed," Patty Anne said. She was smiling a little, so I knew she was kidding. At least, I think so.

"I'm not really a sweater," Eddie said. "Did I mention I'm from Florida?"

"No, I don't believe you mentioned that," I said, salty bullets dripping off my nose. I noticed something as I looked closely at Eddie and Patty Anne. "It could just be the heat making me woozy, but it looks like you two are closer to the surface than when we started," I said.

They looked at each other, then at me. "You too," Patty Anne said.

"Oh boy," Eddie said. "I forgot about the muppies. We need to move faster!"

"Muppies?" I said. "How dangerous can something called muppies be?" Still, I found myself picking up speed without waiting for the answer. I could see the edge of the swamp in the distance, but it was still quite a ways off.

"By themselves, they're not really dangerous," Eddie said, starting to breathe harder as he pushed through the cheese. "They're little mushroom fish that live in the Great Lasagna Swamp. They don't eat people. But here's the problem. Guess what they do eat?"

"Bread," Patty Anne said. "They eat bread! They're eating our stilts! Run!"

As she said that, my left breadstick stilt lurched to one side, and I dropped a couple more inches toward the bubbling sauce. Running wasn't really an option, so I started sliding faster and faster. The edge of the swamp approached with agonizing slowness. I felt like I was in one of those nightmares where you run and run from an unspeakable monster down a long, dark hallway, but you never get any closer to the door at the end.

The muppies were having themselves a feeding

frenzy. They jumped around us, little mushroom-colored, fish-shaped creatures slapping through the air. They bounced off our diminishing breadsticks, snapping off little nibbles each time. My feet were just inches from the lasagna. I could feel the burning sauce when it splashed on my legs. The swamp edge was still yards away. "I'm not going to make it!" I yelled.

"Yes you are! Shut up and move!" Patty Anne screamed.

"Almost there!" Eddie called out.

My right stilt buckled beneath me, and I tumbled forward. Safety was still out of reach. I heaved my left leg in front of me, balanced precariously on the one stilt, spun wildly in a circle, and with a last gasp leaped into the air like I was on a pogo stick. The breadstick stilt bent then straitened out, pulled free of the cheese with a wet sucking sound, and launched me into the air.

Death by lasagna, I thought. *What a way to go.*

CHAPTER 15

eDDIe's STORy

I didn't die, so things were looking up! My toes dragged through the steamy muck at the edge of the swamp, but the rest of me cleared. I landed hard on my side and rolled to a stop. Patty Anne and Eddie managed much more dignified landings than I did, stepping neatly off their crumbling stilts onto dry land. I do mean dry land. It must once have been some sort of meat product but was now as hard, dried and cracked as the floor of Death Valley. Well, that explained the big scrape on my left elbow.

Half a football field away was a mountain riddled with caves. Swiss cheese, I guessed, but this cheese had not been fresh for about a century. It was as parched and cracked as the ground we were standing on, covered in mold and fungus, black with rot in places. Even after several days of carnivorous food and murderous kitchen implements, this was the most unappetizing thing I had seen yet. Somehow, I just knew we were heading straight for those caves. I did see one bright spot, however.

Patty Anne saw it too. "Hey, guys," she said. "Is that a mirage, or do I see a water fountain?"

"Not a mirage," Eddie said. "Every once in a while, Lunch Lady Land surprises you." Halfway between us and the cliffs of moldy cheese was another beautiful school water fountains. I nearly cried from happiness.

Patty Anne and I drank until our bellies could hold no more. The water was colder than a mountain spring and tasted indescribably wonderful. We cleaned up, doused our heads, and scrubbed the accumulated crud from our bodies. By the end of it, I nearly felt human again. Meanwhile, Eddie hung back. He waited until we were done, then drank a little water. He washed himself half-heartedly. He kept glancing at the Swiss cheese mountain, then looking away. Something was definitely wrong.

Patty Anne noticed it too. "Eddie, what is it?" she asked. "Please tell us. Maybe we can help. You've certainly helped us enough."

"She's right," I said. "We're here for you."

Patty Anne looked at me with a smile, her eyes wide. She said, "Josh, that was very sensitive of you."

"Hey, I can be sensitive," I mumbled, slightly embarrassed. Eddie sat down heavily, his back to the water fountain, and sighed deeply. He stared at the mountain for so long that I worried a little. "Eddie?" I said.

He started talking like he hadn't even heard me, in a dull, flat monotone, like all the life had been sucked right out of him. "Cafeteria Castle is on the other side of this mountain, but you can't go over. It's impassable. You have to go through."

I'm pretty sure my gulp was audible, like in a cartoon. "You mean the caves?" I said.

"Yeah, the caves. Those caves lead down into the Catacombs. The Catacombs are one of the most dangerous parts of Lunch Lady Land. There are things down there that make the skybeater look like a teddy bear, things the lunch ladies didn't plan on." He paused for a second, and the next part came out in a whisper. "I don't know if I can get us all through alive."

Patty Anne said, "Are you kidding? After what we've been through, we can handle any—"

"You have no idea!" Eddie yelled, his eyes flashing. Patty Anne and I were so surprised by his outburst that we took a step back. Eddie blushed and looked down. "You have no idea," he said, quieter.

"Eddie, I'm sorry," Patty Anne said.

"No, I'm sorry, I shouldn't have yelled. But there's so much you don't understand. Look, when I told you how I got to Lunch Lady Land, I wasn't completely truthful. I mean, I was, but I left something out."

"Go on," Patty Anne said gently.

"I didn't come here alone," Eddie said.

I heard a "What?!" come out of my mouth before I could stop it. Patty Anne shot me a look that said, *Just let him talk.*

"My twin sister, Debbie, was in the cafeteria with me that day. When I dropped that tray of pudding cups, she rushed over to help me clean up. She told me not to push that button. I didn't listen." Eddie sighed again and it sounded like all the hurt in the world in one little sound. "Debs and I were best friends. It was us against the world. We didn't have anyone else we could count on, anyone else who cared."

"Parents?" Patty Anne asked.

"Not that wanted us," Eddie said, his voice hard all of a sudden. "Anyway. We landed here, the two of us. It was scary at first, as you've both experienced, but we were a great team. We figured things out. We explored and we survived. Then we found our way here, to the Catacombs. We did okay for a while, but we got separated and I … I lost her. She was my sister and I lost her. I spent weeks in the Catacombs, lost, half-crazy, searching for Debs. I almost died a dozen times. By the time I stumbled out of the Catacombs near Cafeteria Castle, it didn't even matter, because I had lost the only thing that mattered to me. The lunch ladies found me and carried me back, to the eggs. So no, I don't know if I can help get you through alive. I'm batting zero for one right now."

Patty Anne reached down and offered Eddie her hand. He shook his head, but he took it and stood up. She said, "I'm willing to take those odds. I can't imagine anyone I'd rather have with me than you and Josh."

I slapped Eddie on the back and said, "You heard the lady. If you're willing, so are we. Let's be honest. We could really use your help." I tried the puppy dog look, which according to my mom hasn't worked for me since I was four, but it was worth a shot.

"All right," Eddie said, and walked toward the Catacombs without looking back.

CHAPTER 16

THE CATACOMBS

I went to school with a kid named Gusty Sullivan who was notorious for never—never ever—washing his gym uniform. By the end of the first semester, a visible cloud of stink would billow out when he opened his locker. The smell burned your nostrils and made your eyes water. By the end of the second semester, Gusty's uniform was actually, literally crunchy. It made a scraping sound like course grain sandpaper when he walked. Random bits flaked off and left a trail behind him, and the smell was a physical presence that draped its arm around you and punched you in the gut when you weren't looking. The Catacombs made Gusty Sullivan's gym uniform smell like a field of roses on a spring morning after a gentle rain. I thought the inside of the canisaur was bad. This was worse by a factor of ten.

Patty Anne and I entered the cave right behind Eddie and immediately stepped into something knee deep and squishy. We had discovered the source of the foul odor. Rotten fruit and vegetables. Not rotten like, "Oh, I'll just cut around the bad parts and enjoy a healthy snack." This was fell-behind-the-fridge-and-didn't-get-noticed-for-three-months rotten, fruit and vegetables the consistency of oatmeal contained in the thinnest of skins. One nudge of your foot and the offending produce burst open.

Patty Anne may have been a monster-tamer, but mushy spoiled fruit was obviously not her favorite thing. She looked a little green around the gills.

"I don't know if I can do this," she said through gritted teeth. "I think I'm going to be sick."

"I feel your pain," I said. "I'm not feeling too perky myself."

Eddie just kept wading through the muck, bloated produce bursting in his wake. He looked back at us, his face pale and frowning, but he managed a small smile. He said, "You know how sometimes things have to get worse before they get better? Well, this is about to get worse, but I promise you it will get better." He stopped abruptly. We were standing at the edge of an enormous, steeply sloping hole in the cave floor, lined with rotten vegetable matter as deep as the eye could see.

"How do we climb down that?" Patty Anne asked.

"We don't," Eddie said. "We slide."

Patty Anne took a step back. "Oh, no," she said. "No way. I'll go around."

Eddie was already shaking his head. "I'm afraid there is no around. This is the only entrance to the Catacombs, at least that I know of."

"Come on, Patty Anne," I said. "Just think of it as a slide after the kindergartners have been on it."

"You know, that actually helps a little," she said.

I guess that was all Eddie needed to hear. He leaped off the edge without another word, landing squarely on what must have once been a giant apple. It exploded, splattering runny innards in every direction. He was soon lost in the darkness below. I held out my hand and Patty Anne took it. We nodded to each other and stepped off together.

I was wrong. This was more like sledding than a slide—except that instead of snow, we slalomed down a river of raw, putrid sewage, and instead of sleds, we rode down on our butts.

"You thought you were dirty before!" I screamed as we slammed into one diseased apple, pear, or carrot after another. Chunks of skin and seeds slapped wetly through the air, hitting us like a hard rain. I closed my eyes and hoped for the best.

"This is not fun!" Patty Anne yelled back at me.

"It's a good thing I'm not still mad, or I'd be blaming you for this!"

"I'm a lucky guy!" I answered. Then a big, shredded sheet of skin smacked me in the face and wrapped around my head, and I spent the next few minutes trying to disentangle myself. Yeah, I said the next few minutes. We slid and rolled for a long, long time. These Catacombs ran deep. I could hear Eddie somewhere below us, sluicing along.

We leveled out at the bottom and kept right on sliding, until the gunk thinned out and we hit the petrified Swiss cheese floor, which did an efficient job of stopping us. Kind of like when you're ice-skating and you reach the end of the ice. I face-planted.

I heard a muffled "Ow!" off to my right, cleaned off my face, and glanced over. Patty Anne looked like the Abominable Rotten-Fruit Man, completely covered in a thick coating of yuck. I started to laugh, but she pointed at me and beat me to it. I looked down and saw that I was just as much of a mess as she was.

I got shakily to my feet and scooped off as much as I could. Patty Anne was doing the same and Eddie was already scraped semi-clean.

"Well, that was just as bad as I remember it," he said. We were in a room-sized cave with the big slide behind us and three tunnels ahead. I was surprised that we could see this deep underground. The cheese walls themselves gave off a faint, greenish light.

"Eddie, why do the walls glow?" I asked.

"I have no idea," he said. "Maybe the cheese diffuses the light or something."

"Probably radioactive," Patty Anne mumbled. She was a little grumpy.

To change the subject I said, "So, do we choose door number one, door number two, or door number three?"

Eddie looked as thoughtful as someone can look with a giant orange seed stuck to the top of his head with fruit pulp. "If memory serves, door number one leads to a bottomless pit."

"How do you know it's bottomless?" I asked, curious.

"Debs"—he winced a little when he said her name—"dropped a big hunk of cheese down it. After an hour or so, it still hadn't hit bottom."

"Okay, so no to door number one. Door number two?"

"Door number two isn't a tunnel. It's a mouth. I was about to step through when Debbie saw it move a little and yanked me back. It snapped shut like an alligator, just missing us. I don't know what's in there, but it almost ate me for lunch."

I stared hard into the shadowed entrance of the second tunnel, feeling goosebumps popping up along my arms and legs. Door number two was definitely out. Patty Anne had been listening closely. "Please tell me door number three isn't carnivorous," she said.

"Nope, not carnivorous," Eddie said. "That's our way forward."

"Is it dangerous?" Patty Anne asked.

Of course it's dangerous, I thought. *This is Lunch Lady Land.*

Eddie had a slightly more hopeful answer. "Not if you're careful," he said. "How do you feel about stalagknives?"

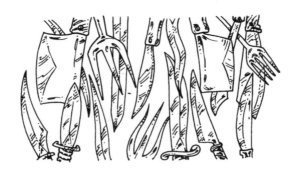

CHAPTER 17

GET THE POINT?

As we duck-walked down the low, narrow tunnel, Patty Anne asked, "Don't you mean stalactites?"

"Or stalagmites?" I added, trying to be helpful. After all, he hadn't been to school in several decades.

"You forget, this is Lunch Lady Land," Eddie said. "I mean stalagknives."

I should have guessed. The tunnel opened out into a cavern filled with razor sharp kitchen implements. A dense mass of oversized knives, cleavers and forks bristled from the cavern ceiling, some of them ten feet long. They jutted from the floor at crazy angles, edges gleaming in the soft light. There was no clear path, just cruel points above and serrated edges below. I saw my grungy face reflected back a thousand times in the polished blades. Like much of Lunch Lady Land, it was equal parts scary and cool.

"So, stalagknives," Patty Anne said. "This is one literal place. What's the plan?"

"Pretty simple, in theory," Eddie said. "Step carefully. Try not to get poked or cut, because I left the first aid kit in my other world. And watch your head. There are a lot of low hanging blades." Eddie had a real gift for understatement. It looked like we were about to take a stroll through one of those medieval iron maiden torture devices.

This time Patty Anne took the lead. She was the most nimble. Surprisingly, I was right behind her. I had joined the Serling Heights wrestling team this season, and it turned out to be good training for navigating a stalagknife-filled cheese cavern. I would have to thank Coach Djerkovich if I ever saw him again. This was all about balance. You had to find a safe place to step and stretch to reach it while simultaneously ducking, bobbing, and weaving so your head didn't become a pincushion. Oh, and you couldn't reach out and grab a knife to steady yourself or you'd lose a finger. Or, you know, an arm.

Patty Anne made the balancing act look graceful, like she was dancing, or doing tai chi. I was going more for athletic than graceful. Whatever worked to keep yourself in one piece.

Eddie seemed to be struggling a little. I was worried he was thinking about his sister and not about cold, steel death. "Hey, Eddie, stay sharp!" I yelled to him. When I realized what I had said I added, "Get the point?"

"Ha ha," he said, but at least it got a smile out of him.

"I'm trying to figure out how to throw one of these knives at you," Patty Anne said. Everyone's a critic.

After executing a complicated step, hop, spin, duck, spin again, and sidestep maneuver, I said, "Wow, I feel like Mario."

"Who's Mario?" Eddie asked. That got a chuckle out of Patty Anne.

"Eddie, I would be honored to introduce you to Mario and his brother Luigi. I hope I get the chance."

"Don't forget Princess Peach," Patty Anne said. "She would rock this place." I thought that Patty Anne was doing a pretty good job of rocking this place herself, but I didn't say it. Wouldn't want her to get a swollen head.

"You two know some interesting people," Eddie said.

"You have no idea," I answered.

We kept on weaving our way through the stalagknives. My arms and legs were nicked up, the top of my head had been poked a couple of times, and my shirt had more holes than the Swiss cheese that surrounded us, but I was okay. Patty Anne and

I were nearing the end of the cavern when I heard a soft thud. A second later Eddie called out, "Hey, guys? I think I need some help."

I looked back and Eddie was gone. No sign of him. "Patty Anne, where's Eddie? I can't find him!" I yelled, my voice squeaky with panic. I hated when that happened.

"There!" she said, pointing. I could see just a hint of his t-shirt. My heart was hammering like a drum line playing the William Tell Overture. We made our way toward Eddie as fast as we could without ending up shish kabobs ourselves.

"I slipped," he said. Eddie had indeed slipped. He was bent over completely backward, his body in an upside-down U shape, his entire weight supported by his toes and fingertips. The small of his back was balanced on the points of three serrated steak knives. If he relaxed for even a microsecond, he'd be skewered like a barbecued pig. Blades on either side prevented him from rolling away. I could see small spots of blood where the knife points pricked him.

"Eddie, I didn't know you were so flexible," I said. Patty Anne punched me in the shoulder, again. "Just trying to keep the mood light."

"That's okay," Eddie said. "I didn't know I was so flexible either. But I'd really like to stand up now."

"All right, buddy, let's see what we can do to help," I said.

"Maybe if we get on either side of him and lift," Patty Anne suggested.

"Works for me." We maneuvered our way into position. We slipped our arms between the knives that surrounded Eddie and managed to clasp hands beneath his shoulders. "Okay," I said, "we're going to lift you up on three." I looked at Patty Anne and she nodded. "One, two, three!"

We heaved. Possibly a little too enthusiastically, because Eddie stood straight up and kept right on going. Eddie was balanced on his tiptoes like a ballet dancer, wheeling his arms, when we both grabbed a handful of shirt and hauled him back. He let out a long breath, like a balloon deflating. "Um, thanks for saving me," he said.

"And almost killing you again?" I added cheerfully.

"No, really, thanks. I got careless. I won't let that happen again."

Patty Anne touched him lightly on the shoulder.

Why doesn't he get punched? I thought.

"It's okay, Eddie," she said. "We're here to help each other."

We quickly—but carefully—worked our way through the remainder of the stalagknives. Another dark tunnel awaited us.

"Hang on a sec," I said. I found a kitchen knife the size of a barbarian's broadsword, grabbed the handle, and wrenched it from the ground. I gave it a couple of experimental swings. "Nice!" I said.

Patty Anne shook her head and said, "This can't end well."

I didn't care what she said, I liked my new sword.

"Hey, it just might come in handy," I said.

Eddie humored me. "Good idea," he said.

We gathered together at the tunnel entrance. I caught a scent and took a deeper sniff. Instead of gagging as usual, my mouth began to water. "Eddie, my friend," I said. "Is that hamburgers I smell?"

CHAPTER 18

CAUGHT IN
THE CURRENT

Up close the smell wasn't nearly as appetizing. We stood next to an underground river of foaming, sputtering hot grease. Huge hamburger boulders split the current, and smaller hamburgers the size of saucer sleds bobbed in the bubbling liquid. More of them were scattered on the shore.

About that particular smell .... There's an all-night place on Serling Heights' main drag called

Dinky's Diner. According to my dad, Dinky hasn't changed his grease since before I was born. I loved Dinky's, despite, or maybe because of, that prehistoric grease scent. No more. I added Dinky's Diner to my ever-growing list of things I would no longer do if I got back home.

Eddie sat down on a hamburger and waved us over. We plopped down on our own burgers. Without thinking about it, I tore off a chunk and started munching. Hey, a guy's got to eat. Plus it tasted exactly like a Dinky's Special.

Eddie's mishap in the stalagknife cavern seemed to have snapped him out of his funk. He jumped right in. "The idea here is that we float down the river on these little burger boats. Obviously the grease is hot, but as long as you stay afloat, it's not bad here. Thing is, the river walls narrow, the current speeds up, and the grease gets rougher. One more thing: the river branches in several places. This is where Debs and I got separated. We have to stay together, no matter what, and I don't know how to make sure that happens."

I jumped up, my mind racing. Well, moving at a fast walk. "Be right back," I yelled over my shoulder as I sprinted for the tunnel to the previous cavern. I was back a few minutes later with an armful of supersized forks and knives. "Let's build us a floating wagon train," I said.

We found three nice-sized hamburgers and attached them in a row using our pile of kitchen weapons, like big, meaty Tinkertoys.

"I like it," Eddie said.

"Nice job, Josh." Patty Anne patted me on the back, which was much nicer than a punch in the shoulder. If this were a movie starring the latest trio of teen heartthrobs, we would have figured out how to attach a rudder for steering. Then again, if we were teen heartthrobs, we wouldn't be covered in rotten food and dried canisaur poop. So no rudder. I had my trusty sword to use as a paddle and push off from boulders, and the other two armed themselves as well.

"Spoons would be better," Patty Anne said, eyeing her skinny steel paddle.

"Spoons are entirely too safe for this place," I answered. "You can't get killed in a cavern filled with spoons."

"Good point," Patty Anne said.

We pushed off into the river, Eddie in front, Patty Anne in the middle, and me bringing up the rear. The burgers were nicely buoyant, riding high in the grease. We paddled a little, mostly to stay perpendicular with the river so we wouldn't smack into a boulder broadside, and let the current carry us deeper into the Catacombs. We avoided collisions with a minimum of poking and paddling.

It was hot and horribly humid on the river. Grease bubbles rose to the surface and burst, spattering us with sizzling drops. Not only did they sting, but I was soon slimier than ever before. "Now I know what a french fry feels like," I said. "I may never look at them the same way again."

"Doesn't matter," Patty Anne said with the conviction of a true believer. "I will always love french fries."

We turned a sharp corner, and the Swiss cheese cliffs on either side of us pinched in. "Here we go," Eddie said. "Get ready to paddle!"

Our boat zigzagged through a series of rapids, picking up speed as we went. The current caught and spun us. We smashed into a burger boulder sideways and nearly tipped before splashing down upright and swirling past. My hamburger was swamped. Grease sprayed across the bottom of my legs, and I jumped to my feet, trying to avoid the hot liquid. If you've ever stood up in a canoe, you know this is a bad idea. I thrust my sword into the burger and used the handle to help balance. I felt like a surfer about to eat a wave. Patty Anne looked back and yelled, "Josh! Stop showing off!"

Why didn't I think of that? We swung hard around

another big boulder, and I dropped to my knees, ignoring the puddles of hot grease. Dead ahead—a phrase I have never liked—the river split into two, the left branch swirling into darkness. The right branch, by the sound of it, boiled over a waterfall. "Hard left!" Eddie shouted above the thunder of tumbling grease. We dug deep with our inadequate paddles, slicing across the current. Our boat slammed into the point where the two branches met, and we slipped left, narrowly avoiding certain death.

My sigh of relief got caught in my throat as we lurched with sickening speed into a narrow, boulder-filled grease stream, bouncing like a pinball, completely out of control. I gave up trying to paddle and just hung on. Directly ahead the river widened out to make room for a whirlpool that sucked us in. We spun faster and faster, caught in the whirlpool's grip. My stomach heaved and I willed myself not to toss my cookies. I curled up in a ball on my little boat, digging my fingers into the meat as centrifugal force tried to pry me loose. Each rotation I caught a glimpse of Eddie and Patty Anne hanging on as best they could.

Our speed seemed to intensify, if that was possible, and we crested the top of the whirlpool. We shot out across the surface of the river, skimming the churning grease, and landed with a splash that threatened to sink us yet again, but our hamburgers held strong. When I realized I was still alive I shouted, "Take that, river! Bring it on!" I didn't care how stupid it sounded, sometimes you just have to shout.

We coasted to a stop in a small eddy between a towering boulder and a cliff wall. I tried to catch my breath. "Eddie, I see why you stay here in Lunch Lady Land," I said. "Never a dull moment."

I was just joking around, but Eddie took it seriously. He said, "Sometimes I ask myself if I've had enough of this, but the truth is, without Debbie I don't want to go back. I'll stick with Lunch Lady Land. Besides, like you said, never a dull moment." He smiled, just a little.

"Speaking of which, we're about to enter the part of the river where Debs and I got separated. It splits and runs into three big tunnels. The river's fast there, and the currents crisscross, so it's hard to steer. Debbie got swept into the left tunnel. I don't know where that leads ... but I heard her screaming." Eddie had to take a minute before he could continue. "I got sucked into the right tunnel. I have at least some idea where that goes, although I got lost pretty quick searching for Debbie. Since I don't know anything at all about the middle tunnel, I think we should shoot for the right."

"Agreed," Patty Anne and I said in unison.

We paddled back into the current and were soon racing along. The tunnels came into view, each as wide as a two-car garage. The grease was really wild here, churning like white water. We immediately bent our backs to the paddles, working toward the right side of the river. We really hit our rhythm, and it looked like smooth sailing. We were doing well.

And then we weren't.

Patty Anne's burger caught on a small boulder jutting out of the grease. The waves spun us like the arms of a clock, with her at the center. When we finally broke loose we were sideways and heading for the middle of the river. "Put some muscle into it!" I said, and we did, but it was already too late. By the time we got our boat straight we were held tight in the middle current. We passed under the edge of the tunnel into deep shadow, and I braced myself for whatever was coming. I told myself to be ready for anything. Then my hamburger boat was gone and I was flying through the air.

This seems to happen to me a lot around here, I thought. While I waited to die, I had one more thought: *Is that cheering I hear?*

CHAPTER 19

CLASH OF THE KITCHENATORS

Jumbo hamburgers may make pretty good boats, but they're not so hot as landing pads. I belly-flopped on my burger boat and felt the air explode out of me with an audible whoosh. Through the little stars and birdies swirling around my head, I saw Patty Anne land butt-first on her burger, bounce twice, and come to a jarring stop. I was worried when Eddie didn't land on his burger, but no problem. He landed on me instead.

As it turned out, there was a short cliff just inside the tunnel mouth, with a deep crevasse at the bottom that sucked away the grease river. We'd been tossed over the edge along with our meat boats, landing in a jumble on the dry, hard cave floor. I pushed Eddie off me and sat up, my head still woozy. Eddie immediately apologized for squishing me.

"No problem," I said. "Glad I could be there to break your fall."

"Don't be a baby," Patty Anne said. She cocked her head. "What's that sound?"

"Sounds like a crowd cheering to me," I said. "Combined with a demolition derby. But that's silly, even for Lunch Lady Land. Eddie?"

Eddie shook his head. "We're in uncharted territory here. I have no idea."

"Then let's go find out," Patty Anne said.

We belly-crawled through a low, jagged hole in the wall, then had to crawl down a tunnel so long that my knees were screaming for mercy by the time there was room to stand. The sound got louder all the while. Piercing metal on metal crashes were followed by unhinged screaming. The tunnel finally widened out and we could see the hint of a cavern ahead. We crept quietly to the opening and peeked in.

None of us spoke for several minutes. Myself, I just let the weird wash over me.

Eddie was the first to break the silence. "This is new," he said.

Patty Anne broke into a huge smile and said, "This is so totally cool."

I could feel myself smiling just as big, but I was rendered inarticulate by the awesome display before me and barely managed a mumbled "Wow."

We were looking at a vast coliseum hewn from the cheese. At the center, facing each other like gladiators, stood a giant potato peeler and an equally monolithic cheese grater. They had thick, sturdy metal legs and useless little T. rex arms. Surrounding them in tier after tier of box seats that climbed to dizzying heights were their fellow graters to one side and peelers to the other.

Now, I know what you're thinking. Oversized kitchen accessories, whoopty-do. Let me try to explain. You know how, in cheesy sci-fi movies from the fifties, if they wanted something to appear scary, they just made it bigger? Tarantulas, chameleons, bunny rabbits, supersized and rampaging through the countryside. This was like that, taken to a ridiculous extreme.

The kitchenators, as I immediately began to think of them, were at least thirty feet tall, scarred metal monsters with wicked sharp faces. They circled each other warily, stomping their feet like sumo wrestlers. The crowd thundered with guttural, metallic cheers. The peelers jeered at the graters. The graters hooted at the peelers. They all did the wave with their tiny little arms. Then the warriors launched themselves at each other with a mighty roar. Metal teeth ripped against metal blades with a sound like a hundred-car pile-up. Sparks fountained into the air as they ground against each other, digging in their heels for leverage. They tore away from each other, staggered back a few steps, and began to circle again. The crowd shook the cavern with their frenzied cheers.

"Can we stay here for a while?" I asked hopefully. "I can watch this all day."

"Me too," Patty Anne said. "But I think we should keep moving. I want to go home." Sure, those were the words coming out of her mouth, but when the kitchenators slammed into each other again, her eyes were glued to the show.

"As entertaining as this is, I agree with Patty Anne," Eddie said. "Let's try to get you guys home."

Fine. One problem, though. There was no way to cross the coliseum floor without being seen, and we had no idea if the big fellas were friendly. "Slow and

149

steady, or make a run for it?" I asked.

"Let's try slow and steady to start, and see what happens," Patty Anne said. We set out around the rim of the coliseum like we were going on a Sunday stroll. I focused my eyes like laser beams on the cave opening across the cavern floor. I tried to look casual, but each time the kitchenators clashed, I just about jumped out of my skin.

"How are we doing?" I whispered.

"I think okay," Eddie said. "They're ignoring us so far." We kept as far away from the battling beasts as we could, but that meant we were closer to the crowd. That worked fine until we were two thirds of the way around. That's when a potato peeler in the bottom tier of seats noticed us. It glanced at us, looked up at the battle, then glanced down at us again, like a human seeing a spider on the ground for the first time and trying to decide whether to step on it. It stopped cheering.

"Uh-oh," Patty Anne said. "We may have a problem."

"Just keep walking," Eddie said. "Maybe it'll forget about us."

The peeler stood up and leaned forward, towering over us. It pointed one T. rex finger directly at us, and it shrieked like a pod person from *Invasion of the Body Snatchers*. We were made.

"Run!" I yelled.

We ran. More of the crowd noticed us and joined in the shrieking. The kitchenators realized they had lost the crowd and turned in our direction. *Typical divas,* I thought. *They don't want to share the spotlight.* Then I wasn't thinking anything at all as I turned on the jets in an all-out sprint for the exit, the two giants teaming together to give chase. The ground shook with mini cheesequakes as they closed in on us. Eddie and Patty were right with me. The cave mouth was tantalizingly close. Some of the crowd even cheered for us. Either that or they were cheering for our imminent demise, but I decided to stay positive.

The cheese grater launched itself high into the air.

Oh, grate, I thought. I meant great. *We're about to be squished and grated at the same time.*

Its shadow passed over us, dropping fast. I leaned forward, stretching for the cave. I saw Patty Anne and Eddie's feet disappear into the opening, and a little part of my brain thought, *Good. They made it.* The rest of my brain screamed, *Nooooooooooooooooooooo!* as round metal blades ripped down my back.

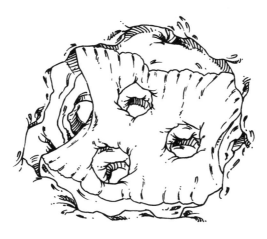

CHAPTER 20

ONe BaD aPPLe

"My mom is not going to be happy about this," I said, the shredded remains of my shirt in my hands. "Oh well. At least I didn't get grated like parmesan." I shrugged back into it, although it seemed a little pointless.

"That was a close one," Eddie said.

"But still really cool," Patty Anne added. She looked

back, I think a little longingly, at the kitchenators who were facing off again. We were already forgotten. That's showbiz, I guess.

I took a good look at our surroundings. Basic cave, except for being made of old, dried-out cheese. "I like it right here," I said. "Nothing in the immediate vicinity appears to want to kill us."

"I'm sure we can fix that," Patty Anne said. We moved on. Patty Anne and Eddie had abandoned their swords during our flight to safety, but I still had mine. I hefted it as we walked, comforted by the weight. We were soon circling through a series of spiral tunnels and switchbacks, climbing steep rises and skidding down drop-offs. Nothing jumped out at us, or swept us away, or jabbed us with pointy things. It was almost relaxing after what we'd been through.

The cave began to change. Tunnels were broken in places and we had to squeeze through the gaps. The floor tilted at crazy angles and cheese slides sometimes blocked our way. We had to double back and find a new path several times. "Something happened here," Eddie said. "Something big."

"I just hope that something isn't hungry," I said.

"I think Eddie was speaking more geologically than predatory. Some sort of cataclysm happened here."

I turned a blind corner and smacked face first into our cataclysm. An apple the size of a barn had dropped down, with unimaginable force, into the Catacombs. It had done geological violence when it happened, the damage rippling out from the impact site in the waves of destruction we'd been traveling through. That had been a long time ago. The apple was now part of the cave system, the once bright red skin dusty and rotten, peeled away in spots, the meat of the apple hard and spotted with brown.

One other thing of note. Huge tunnels, perfectly round and large enough to walk through upright, had been bored through the apple. I poked the tunnel entrance with my sword. Something thin and slimy coated the tip and I wiped it on my jeans. "So, Eddie, Patty Anne ... what do you suppose made these nice round tunnels?"

"That is an interesting question," Patty Anne said. "But this overgrown apple is standing between us and freedom, so I'm going to pretend you didn't ask it."

The apple was easy going. The slime I had noticed at the opening was everywhere, but the tunnels were smooth and firm, nice for walking. And there were lots of them. They riddled the apple, intersecting, rising, and falling. At each intersection, we chose the direction that seemed right and always picked up instead of down.

Eddie was in the lead when he stopped dead, causing a three-kid pileup. I nearly skewered Patty Anne with my sword. Another tunnel crossed ours just ahead. "Why'd you stop?" I asked.

Eddie held up one hand. "Shhh. I thought I heard something."

"Like what?" Patty Anne asked.

"I'm not sure," he said. "Like a swooshy sound."

Swooshy. Right. I was mentally rolling my eyes when a worm that barely fit swooshed through the tunnel ahead of us, its sides moist and gooey. The three of us froze. I held my breath as the worm—a whole lot of worm—slid by. When I finally had to take a breath or risk passing out, the worm was still passing through.

"It's like waiting for a train," Patty Anne whispered.

"At least now we know what made these tunnels," Eddied whispered back.

The worm's tail slipped out of sight. Do worms have tails? They're kind of all tail, when you think about it. Anyway, the worm was gone. "Let's go," Eddie said, still whispering.

When we stepped into the cross tunnel, the worm was sitting there, end swishing back and forth.

"Move!" Eddie yelled. No need to whisper now. We sprinted down the tunnel. The worm, its fat, round body slick with slime, snaked around the corner and headed in our direction. The worm was fast. We managed to keep some distance, but not much, by switching direction at each intersection. The big guy didn't corner well. Unfortunately I was starting to get winded.

We hit a hub where three tunnels came together, and another worm joined the hunt. "Of course there's more than one," I managed to say between gasps. "Man, I'm getting tired."

"Me too," Patty Anne said.

"We need to think of something," Eddie said. "I'm not going to last much longer."

A few seconds later the apple made the decision for us. We hit a dead end. There was another tunnel, but it went straight up. "Time to make a stand!" I said. "I was getting tired of running anyway." I held my sword at the ready. "Get behind me." I hoped my voice wasn't squeaking.

The worm came around the corner. It completely

filled the tunnel. Man, it was big. I grasped the sword handle with both hands, willing them to stop shaking. Patty Anne and Eddie stood behind me, ready to fight. The worm kept coming. "Get ready," I said.

Then I heard a voice from the tunnel above us. "Hey, kid! You, with the red hair. Yeah, you! Put down the sword and step away from the worm!"

CHAPTER 21

REUNION

"Move back, I'm coming down!" the voice yelled. It was rough and croaky, like it hadn't been used in a long while. We did as we were told, equal parts shell-shocked and curious. Plus, I don't know about the others, but it kept my mind off the worm hovering nearby. I heard a flapping sound in the tunnel above, a whoosh, and then a wild creature landed in a crouch between us.

"Debbie!" Eddie screamed.

"Eddie!" Debbie croaked. They hugged for about half a day while Patty Anne and I looked on with big, stupid grins. Debbie had gone native. She had Eddie's lanky blonde hair, but it hung in dreadlocks, wrapped in ribbons made from vegetable strings. She still had remnants of her original clothes, shorts and a t-shirt, but they were patched and decorated with woven cloth made from the same strings. A belt around her waist held handmade tools and odds and ends. Debs was apparently as handy as her brother.

Eddie pulled back, held Debbie at arm's length. "I thought you were dead," he said. He had tears in his eyes, but he was smiling. "I am so, so sorry we got separated. I spent weeks looking for you, but I never found a trace. I promise I will never lose you again."

She hugged him again, tightly. "It wasn't your fault," she said. "I looked for you too. When I finally gave up, it felt like I was turning my back on you. I'm sorry."

"Why didn't you try to escape the Catacombs?" Eddie asked. I have to admit, I was wondering the same thing. The Catacombs made the rest of Lunch Lady Land seem downright cheery.

"I did try, at least at first. But without you my heart wasn't really in it. And the one way out I found is too dangerous. I didn't think I could make it by myself." Debbie looked pretty tough, so I didn't like the sound of that.

"You're not by yourself now, not anymore."

Eddie seemed to realize that we were standing there like fools, watching their reunion. "Debbie, these are my new friends. I'm helping them get to the Lunch Ladies."

Debbie couldn't stop smiling. "Wait, let me guess," she said. "Dorothy and the Tin Man."

"Oh, I like her!" Patty Anne said. She reached out her hand for Debbie to shake. "I'm Patty Anne. Your brother here has saved our skins half a dozen times."

"Hi, I'm Josh," I said. "Thanks for making me the Tin

162

Man, and not the Cowardly Lion or the Scarecrow."

"No problem," she said.

Eddie put his arms around both our shoulders and said, "If it weren't for these two, I would never have found you again. I owe them everything. I'm going to do everything I can to help them get home."

"I'm ready to help. I think I've spent enough time here in the Catacombs. I could do with some sunshine, even if it is fluorescent."

"Say, Debbie," I said. "Not to change the subject, but what's the deal with ... them? They were trying to eat us." I pointed a thumb at the killer worm. Its buddy was hanging out farther down the tunnel.

Debbie reached right out and scratched the worm on its slimy tip. Its whole body wiggled like it was wagging its tail. Now I felt stupid for being afraid of it. "These are my friends," she said. "They weren't trying to eat you. They don't even have teeth. They're kind of like overgrown puppies. You should see them play fetch. I named this one Bob. That one down there is Harry, because he looks like my Uncle Harry."

"He does look like Uncle Harry," Eddie said.

Debbie got a serious look on her face. "They've kept me company for all these years, and a lot of the other creatures down here are afraid of them because they're so big. I'm not sure I would have survived without them."

"Then they're my friends too," Eddie said. He gave the worm a tentative pat.

"I think they're cute," Patty Anne said, but she didn't pet the beast, just gave it a little half wave.

Debbie squared her shoulders and nodded her head, like she had just made a decision. "If we're going, I need to say goodbye to the worms. Especially Bob and Harry, they're my favorites." She spread her arms wide and wrapped them around Bob. She whispered something that I couldn't hear, then kissed him right on what would have been his nose, if worms had noses. Her face was thoroughly slimed when she let go, but she didn't seem to mind at all.

Debbie repeated this with Harry, and with several other worms that had gathered in nearby tunnels without me realizing it. She hiked back to us, covered in worm goop but smiling. "I'm going to miss these guys," she said. "They're not much for conversation, but it was comforting having them around. I slept every night cuddled up against them and I knew nothing would get me in my sleep."

Debbie gave Eddie another hug, transferring some of her newly acquired slime. "I am so glad you found me. Now let's go see those lunch ladies," she said. We set off, a much happier, and slightly larger, group than when we had entered the Catacombs. Debbie whistled softly as we hiked, and I laughed when I recognized the tune: "We're Off to See the Wizard."

CHAPTER 22

POP GOES THE JOSH

"Popcorn! I love popcorn!" I said with relief. I was staring into a large cavern filled with popcorn as big as basketballs. In one corner, bright flames climbed the wall and popcorn spewed out of the fire. The popcorn flowed across the floor of the cavern as more and more popped, the kernels jostling together gently. This was the reason Debbie had stayed in the Catacombs? Popcorn?

The past couple of days had been challenging, but

the four of us were a good team. Debbie was a good guide, and she had explored a lot of the surrounding caves and tunnels. She knew which caverns we should absolutely avoid and which ones we had to chance. As a bonus, she was fun to be around, funny, and a little sarcastic. She and Eddie were both so happy they had reunited.

We battled a tribe of bowling ball-sized onions with eight little spider legs. They were scary at first, but we quickly found their Achilles heel. When you kicked them hard, their layers burst open and the mini centers ran away screaming. They did make my eyes water, though. We sped at breakneck speed through a long tunnel lined on both sides with ancient, rusted toasters. A blizzard of burned toast pelted us as we ran. We tried to duck and weave, but it was like trying to run between raindrops. We finally gave up and took the hits, moving as fast as possible. I could already feel the bruises by the time we reached the end.

We had to swim to the top of a vertical tunnel filled with ginger ale. That one was kind of fun. The bubbles poured up from the bottom, spinning me around, tickling my skin. I felt lighter than air in the bubble stream, like I was in space, floating in zero gravity. I was almost disappointed when I finally broke the surface. At least until I started to dry, when the ginger ale turned sticky and my skin began to itch.

The worst we faced came in a small room that Debbie had never entered. Thick strands of what looked like sausage casings hung from the ceiling, waving slightly in a soft breeze that we couldn't feel, like jellyfish suspended under water. We stepped in and a shiver ran through the tattered, translucent casings, like they knew we were there. A casing brushed my shoulder and a shock of electricity jolted through me, then another. The other three yelped simultaneously as they came in contact. "Drop to the ground!" I yelled.

We crawled along the floor, avoiding most of the sausage skins. But some of them hung all the way to the bottom, and I swear the tendrils reached for us. I was stung over and over, sharp little shocks that sent ripples of pain through my body. When the four of us tumbled into the tunnel at the end of the cavern, my arms and legs were barely working. We collapsed, moaning, waiting for our limbs to begin responding again. All of us were covered in hot red welts.

Now we faced a room full of popcorn. "I love popcorn!" I said again for emphasis. "Let's go."

Debbie grabbed me by the collar and yanked me back before I could take a step. "Slow down there, cowboy," she said. "Looks easy, doesn't it? Watch." She broke off a piece of cave cheese and tossed it into the room. When it hit a plump piece of popcorn it exploded with a startling roar, setting off a chain reaction of other kernels. New popcorn soon drifted into the area. "And that," she said, "is why I'm still in here. Touch a kernel and pop goes the Josh. See how the popper in the corner there keeps popping new popcorn bombs? I tried to clear a path by exploding them, but they kept moving around, and there was no way to watch my own back ...."

"But with four of us," Eddie jumped in, "we can watch each other's backs and keep the bombs at bay."

"Exactly."

"Works for me," Patty Anne said.

"Looks like we all need some ammunition," I said. We got busy excavating chunks of the walls, filling pockets and then using the fronts of our shirts. When we were armed, we gathered at the entrance. "Let's stay in a circle," I said. "Keep a safe distance around us. Okay, bombs away!" We lobbed our ammo in, and the explosions were deafening. We moved forward together in a tight circle, backs together. New popcorn rolled in like lethal tumbleweeds. We tossed our chunks, meeting each bomb, and kept moving. Explosions rocked the walls. Small bits of cheese rained down on us like little rockslides.

We were near the end of the cavern when a piece of popcorn slipped by my defenses. I chucked some cheese at it way too late and the blast blew me off my feet, knocking me into Eddie and causing our own chain reaction. We all went down, hard. The popcorn bombs crept closer. "Keep throwing!" Patty Anne yelled. My ears were ringing so badly her voice was muffled. We climbed shakily to our feet, clearing space. The explosions were still a little close for comfort. I could feel the shock waves.

We made it. I dropped to the ground, my head throbbing. I felt my ears, afraid I'd find blood. That list of things I would never again do? Eating popcorn was now on it. If I ever got back home, my life was going to be very boring. "That was not fun," I said. My own voice sounded far away.

Patty Anne was sitting next to me. "Hey, Josh," she said and I could now hear her a little better. "There's something you need to see." She leaned back so I could see past her. We were in a long, narrow tunnel.

At the far end, just visible, was a circle of daylight.

I practically ran down that tunnel, the others right behind me. When I stumbled out of the Catacombs, tears blurred my eyes. I tried and failed to fight them back. "I have never been so happy to see a big, fluorescent sun," I said. The others were dealing with happy tears of their own. I found myself engulfed in a group hug.

Our hug was soon interrupted by a familiar voice inside my head. *It's about time you got here. I've been waiting for days! By the way, who's your friend?*

CHAPTER 23

aTTacK OF THE
LUNCH LaDIes

"Skybaby!" Patty Anne yelled as she ran to hug the skybeater.

When Debbie saw her former nemesis, she pulled a wicked looking homemade knife from her belt and took off at a dead run, eyes blazing.

"Uh-oh," Eddie said, and we both shot after her. Now we were all running.

Patty Anne reached the skybeater first. When she turned and saw Debbie, she stepped in front of her and held up both hands. "Stop! Stop! Please don't hurt her!"

Debbie pulled up short her face red. "Don't hurt her? What do you mean, don't hurt her? She's a monster! Do you know what she's done?" Eddie and I reached Debbie, and we each put a hand on her shoulder, partly to comfort her and partly to hold her back.

Eddie talked quietly to her, trying to calm her down. "Debbie, the skybeater has changed. She's a reformed monster, and she's promised never to attack the eggs again. She never wanted to be mean to begin with, but that's how the lunch ladies programmed her."

"She promised? What, did she tell you she'd be good from now on?" Debbie's arms were tightly crossed and the expression on her face was equal parts furious and skeptical.

"Well, yes," Eddie said. "She promised all of us. She can talk, sort of." Eddie looked at the skybeater. "Skybeater, I sound like a fool here. Can you just go ahead and do your thing?"

Debbie's face was amazing to watch as the skybeater began talking to her telepathically. She looked confused at first, spinning in a circle, searching for the source of the voice in head. You could see the anger drain away as she listened and finally accepted that the monster of her nightmares was talking to her, telling her that it had changed. I knew things would be okay when Debbie took the knife she'd been holding with white knuckles and slipped it back into her belt.

"Um, guys?" she said. "She says ... the skybeater says she would be honored to give us a ride to the lunch ladies." Debbie shook her head. "This is so crazy."

Eddie said, "Debs, I know this is a shock. Believe me. It was a shock to me too. Are you on board with this?"

"I trust you with my life," she said. "If you say

it's okay, then it's okay. I have to admit, Lunch Lady Land is full of surprises."

"That it is."

Patty Anne looked relieved that Debbie had accepted the situation. She turned her attention to the skybeater. "Are you sure you can carry us? That canisaur really did a number on you."

I heard the skybeater's answer, and by their faces, I figured the rest did as well. *Please, it takes more than that to knock down this old bird. If Eddie and his hotdog slingshot hasn't killed me yet, what chance does an overgrown tin can have? And Debbie? I want everyone to hear me say, once more, how sorry I am for the pain I caused you in the past. Now, if we're all good, climb aboard!*

We all crawled onto the skybeater's back and found handholds. The rotors coughed and sputtered, then caught and revved up to full speed. We lurched into the air. It seemed like we were tilting a little to the left, but otherwise the skybeater was flying strong. The Catacombs soon disappeared behind us, much to my delight, and we flew over a flat, featureless plain that was the uniform brown color of old shoe leather—so it was probably made from meat of some sort.

When we passed over some low meatloaf foothills, Eddie sat up and said, "Okay, now, look straight ahead. We'll be coming up on Cafeteria Castle."

"There!" Patty Anne said, pointing. "Something shiny."

Fluorescent sunlight sparkled brightly off a spot on the horizon.

Cafeteria Castle soared into the sky where the foothills began to give way to higher mountains. It was all stainless steel, from the high, arching walls to the pointed spires at the tops of towers. Stainless steel battlements climbed to impossible heights. Silver flags snapped in the breeze.

"Oh, wow," Patty Anne said. "I can't believe the lunch ladies ever want to leave here."

"Are you kidding?" Eddie said. "They're never really happy unless they're dropping spoonfuls of mystery stew on a cafeteria tray. That's what they live for." Eddie was interrupted by a *twang* sound so loud we could hear it over the racket the skybeater made. It came from the direction of the castle.

"Now what?" I asked.

I had my answer a second later when a pizza the size of a minivan spun past us.

"Uh-oh," Eddie said.

"Uh-oh what?" Another *twang* and another pizza came spinning our way, this one much closer.

"They can't see us. They think the skybeater is coming to mess with them!"

"You mean ...?"

"The lunch ladies are attacking!"

CHAPTER 24

SUPER KUCHEN

"Under attack again," Patty Anne said. "Man, this is getting old! Come on, Skybeater. Time to take evasive maneuvers." The skybeater was way ahead of Patty Anne. She banked sharply to the left and down, then cut back around in a big figure eight. Pizzas sliced past us like deadly Frisbees. The skybeater weaved and spun like a rabbit escaping a wolf. There was nothing we could do but hang on.

"We can't keep dodging pizzas all day!"

"We have to get close enough for the lunch ladies to see us," Eddie said. Then he got a big smile on his face, which seemed a little odd under the circumstances.

"Something funny about this?" I asked.

Eddie swallowed a laugh. "No, not funny at all. But the skybeater just sent me a message. She said, 'How about we all climb on *your* back and *you* fly us closer to the lunch ladies.'"

"Everybody's a comedian. Even giant flying kitchen tools."

"But she has a point," said Patty Anne.

"Okay, I get it," Eddie said. He patted the skybeater on her side. "Just do your best, please."

The lunch ladies found their range. A pizza shot over us so close it blew back my hair. The next was a solid hit, right in the beaters. Chunks of crust, cheese, and sauce hit us in a gloopy spray. Sploosh! Another hit! The skybeater rocked, bouncing me hard.

The pizzas slammed us like machine gun fire. The skybeater's rotors sputtered. We dropped fifty feet in half a second before we leveled out. I added roller coasters to my list of things I was giving up if we ever got home.

"She can't stay in the air much longer!" Patty Anne screamed. "We're not going to make it!"

A message from the skybeater poked its way into my head. *Don't count me out yet, kids! This isn't my first rodeo! Hold on tight!* We dropped into a nosedive so steep we felt the g-forces. The ground rushed up at us. I was starting to sweat a little when we pulled up hard, skimming right along the surface, banking left and right. The lunch ladies couldn't get a bead on us zipping back and forth at such a low altitude. Pizzas whizzed by far over our heads and smashed into the ground. "I'm starting to like this skybeater!" Debbie yelled.

The ground flew below us in a blur as the shimmering base of Cafeteria Castle rushed to meet us. Just before smashing to bits against the stainless steel wall, we ripped into a climb parallel to the castle. I clung to the skybeater's back, grimly holding on, terrified I'd drop to my death. I could see our reflection mirrored in the wall as we skipped along at breakneck speed.

The bottom of a balcony appeared above us. We slowed down, looped out, and dropped onto the balcony with a horrible clatter of metal on metal, finally skidding to a stop. The rotors had dug gouges in the balcony floor.

Then strong hands grabbed the back of my shirt and yanked me off the skybeater. I heard cries of "Hey!" and "What gives?" from my companions, so I knew they had been scooped up too. The skybeater revved back up and leaped into the air. I felt a faint *Good luck* in my mind as she flew away.

What strange creature had a firm grip on my shirt? I twisted around and strained my neck to see. "Mrs. Kuchen!" I yelled simultaneously with Patty Anne.

I was looking up into the face of Lunch Lady Kuchen. At least, some version of Lunch Lady Kuchen. She had big white wings like an eagle, for one thing. She was smiling, which was definitely new. Her uniform was so clean and shiny it glowed, and her hairnet looked like a golden crown. She seemed almost like a superhero. Super Kuchen. Way cool. Plus she was flying, which Lunch Lady Kuchen couldn't do, as far as I knew. She unceremoniously dumped the four of us on the balcony floor.

"You children are very resourceful," she said. "I'm not sure how you managed to tame the skybeater, but my colleagues are going to be rather unhappy. Personally, I'm impressed."

"Hello," Eddie said. I guess he wasn't quite as surprised by Super Kuchen's appearance.

"Eddie Eggs, nice to see you again. It's been a while. Josh, Patty Anne, glad to see you made it this far. We lost track of you and we were growing worried. And is that Miss Kowalski? Oh, my goodness." Tears appeared in the corners of her eyes and even they glistened like precious jewels. "We thought we had lost you, my dear. I am so very glad to see you ... and so very glad we did not manage to shoot you out of the sky."

Debbie suddenly seemed shy. "I'm glad about that too, ma'am."

Lunch Lady Kuchen folded her wings. Her smile was brighter than the sunlight reflecting off Cafeteria Castle. "Follow me, kids. I'll answer your questions as we walk." In the quiet of the castle interior, her voice sounded like music.

We shuffled through an endless maze of shiny, perfect corridors. It looked like a hotel designed by scientists specifically for astronauts. Other lunch ladies passed us. They smiled and ruffled our hair on the way by. Normally, I would find this majorly annoying, but with them I didn't mind. Eddie greeted some by name. Some of them stopped dead in their tracks when they saw Debbie and wrapped her in enormous lunch lady hugs. She didn't seem to mind that.

I was too overwhelmed at first to ask any questions. Not good old Patty Anne, though. "First things first …. Why are we here?"

"By accident, I'm afraid. Some older schools, like yours and Mr. and Miss Kowalski's, have long-forgotten emergency portals. We seal them up as we find them. Sometimes kids discover them before we do."

"Kids like us."

"Yes, dear. Kids like you."

We peeked inside open doors as we passed. There were kitchens as big as football fields, gleaming with chrome and stainless steel. There were cafeterias the size of the Grand Canyon, with acres of Formica and polished tile. Lunch ladies buzzed about everywhere. They cooked, manned the line, carried trays.

"Training," Mrs. Kuchen said before we even asked.

"All the crazy, dangerous stuff here—ladle people, spoonies, canisaurs, the skybeater—more training?" Patty Anne asked.

"Yes, indeed. Advanced combat training, in fact. Once you've faced off against the skybeater, a surly eighth grader is a picnic. Once you've experienced the Catacombs, a lunch table full of kindergartners shoving food down their shirts doesn't seem so bad."

"Mrs. Kuchen," I said, "I don't mean to be rude, but I have to ask. Why are you so different here than in school?"

"Not rude at all, Josh. You see, this is my true self, me at my very best. My ideal. But it wouldn't do to have me flying about your school, glowing."

We came to an elevator at the end of the corridor and got in. Mrs. Kuchen pushed the LL button. We started dropping, fast. "So," Patty Anne said, "in our world you have to be more ... human."

"Exactly."

"And more grumpy," I said without thinking. Open mouth, insert foot.

Patty Anne caught me in the ribs with a sharp elbow, but Mrs. Kuchen just laughed. "Yes, Josh, I am grumpy. And mean. It's all part of the job. Grumpiness causes friction and friction builds character. Our goal is to make each of you a better person, and surviving adversity does that. So, we provide a little bit of adversity every day at lunch time."

I decided to go for broke. "What about the bad food? What's the point of training lunch ladies to cook if all they make for us is slop?"

She laughed again and it sounded like bells ringing. "More character building. We can't make things too cushy. You see, my fellow lunch ladies aren't learning to cook well here. They are being taught the fine art of taking perfectly nutritious food and making it taste horrible. Not an easy task!"

"I knew it!" Patty Anne said. "No one can cook that bad by accident!" She paused and bit her lower lip. When she spoke again, her voice was much more serious. "Um, Mrs. Kuchen? This has been an amazing experience. Scary, but amazing. But are we going home soon?"

As she said it, I realized how much I wanted to go home too. "Yeah, just point us toward that little door."

"I'm afraid it's not quite that easy." Uh-oh. The elevator coasted to a stop. "How do you kids feel about jello?

CHAPTER 25

IN DEEP JeLLO

I hate jello. It's not the taste. I don't mind that. It's the texture. There's something about the wiggling, slippery stuff that ooks me out. So when Lunch Lady Kuchen asked about jello, the alarm bells starting ringing in my head. The alarm bells turned to police sirens after the elevator doors opened.

Round bowls of jello as big as baby pools were set into the spotless metal floor. Thousands of them, in neat rows, disappeared into the distance. The air was chilly, and had an unmistakable smell. I saw every color imaginable, and a few I didn't recognize. Red, green, blue, orange, yellow—on and on, without any pattern I could see.

"That," said Patty Anne, "is a whole lot of jello!"

Lunch Lady Kuchen consulted a small notebook. "This way, kids." She glided forward and we followed. Our footsteps caused the pools to jiggle as we passed.

"I don't like jello," I whispered to Patty Anne, "and I don't think I'm going to like this."

Patty Anne sighed at me. Loudly. "Josh, come on. After everything we've been through? How bad can it be?" Famous last words all over again. Eddie laughed. He had been very quiet since reaching Cafeteria Castle, hanging back. His laugh surprised me.

Mrs. Kuchen checked her notebook again and said, "Oh, drat!" We turned around and backtracked three rows, then continued in a new direction.

"Spill it," I said to Eddie. "What do you know?"

He laughed again. "Well, I have been offered this opportunity before. So let me put it this way. Are you a strong swimmer?"

"Oh, no—"

Lunch Lady Kuchen stopped suddenly. Patty Anne bumped into her, and I bumped into Patty Anne. Eddie and Debbie brought up the rear. Sort of like the caboose in a train wreck.

Mrs. Kuchen pretended we hadn't ruffled her wings. "And here we are." We were standing next to a pool of bright orange jello. Oversized chunks of fruit floated in it. I especially didn't like orange jello with fruit in it.

"Getting in and out of Lunch Lady Land is simple for us lunch ladies. For you, however, it's a little more complicated. Some of the portals, while perfectly safe for us, would do things to your body I'd prefer not to describe." Patty Anne looked a little pale. My tongue felt like sandpaper.

"Which brings us to this place. The jello room. Each of these pools corresponds to a cafeteria in your world. One for each. This one connects to yours. Traveling through the portal is not entirely pleasant, but it won't kill you."

"That's ... reassuring," I said.

"If you say it's safe, we trust you," Patty Anne said.
She shot me a look like my mom does sometimes.
"Don't we, Josh?"

"Um, yeah, sure. I guess."

Mrs. Kuchen put a hand on each of our shoulders. A sense of peace flowed over me, like hot fudge on a sundae. "You can do this. Just dive in, swim for the bottom, and keep on swimming. No harm will come to you."

"Okay," Patty Anne said. "But wait a minute. What about Eddie and Debbie?"

Eddie, that's right! "Yeah! Eddie, you can go home now. The skybeater promised to leave the eggs alone."

Mrs. Kuchen looked at Eddie with a funny expression. "How about it, Mr. Kowalski? Miss Kowalski? Would you like to return home? Your own jello pool is just a few rows over."

Eddie didn't answer for a long time. "I don't

know," he finally said. "This has been my home for so long, I'm afraid I won't know how to act back in the world."

Debbie took Eddie's hands in hers. "Eddie, I know it's scary, but I'd like to go back. I think maybe I'd like to try growing up. Look, I know there's still no one back there for us, but that's okay. We found each other again and together we can handle anything."

"Debs, I am so glad to have you back in my life that, if this is what you want, I'll do it," Eddie said. "But I'm terrified the real world will be even scarier than Lunch Lady Land."

"You're the bravest guy I know," Debbie said.

Eddie smiled and said, "Let's go home."

Mrs. Kuchen smiled. "That's fine, kids. Just fine." She looked at us. "You two first. It's time, dears."

Eddie and Debbie hugged us both. We'd only known him for several days, and Debbie even less, but man, what days! I had a catch in the back of my throat. Patty Anne had tears in her eyes.

We stood at the lip of the pool. "I'm ready to go home," Patty Anne said.

"Let's get this over with," I said.

Mrs. Kuchen wrapped her wing tips around us. "Good luck. Oh, one more thing. Very important. You must not speak of this, to anyone. And when you see me back in school, it will be like none of this ever happened. I'll be my usual, grumpy self. Got it?"

"Got it. Like anyone would believe us." I took a couple of deep breaths and looked over at Patty Anne.

"Hey," she said, "bet I beat you to the finish line."

"You're on."

I dove in.

Cold! The jello was cold and slippery. I commanded my teeth not to chatter and started stroking. Let me tell you: jello is not made for swimming. I felt like I was moving in slow motion. I pushed my arms forward and scooped back, frog-kicking my feet.

I was afraid to open my eyes in the gunk, so I swam blind. My head kept bumping into basketball-sized pieces of fruit. I had this terrible thought. What if I get turned around and swim the wrong way? I dug faster. My arms and legs felt like they were on fire.

There was no end to it. Maybe Lunch Lady Kuchen was really a psycho. She was up there laughing maniacally as I drowned in a wiggly orange dessert. With fruit.

Pain filled my chest. I was light-headed, having trouble concentrating. Fireworks exploded behind my eyelids. My arms were so tired. I needed to stop and rest, maybe take a little nap. Yeah, a little nap would be just the ticket. And a great big breath of air. Jello. Whatever. I opened my mouth wide.

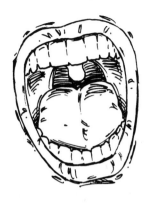

CHAPTER 26

Back to Normal?

I sucked in a mouthful of jello. I started choking. This is it, I thought. Drowning is no fun at all. It took me a second to realize I was still alive and breathing in air along with the orange glops. I waited for the hacking to stop, then opened my eyes.

I was back in the Serling Heights Intermediate School cafeteria, sitting in a big tray of orange jello on the lunch line. My reappearance had made a huge mess, splashing jello everywhere. Assorted food slime from three days in Lunch Lady Land coated my body. I slid half a cherry off my nose and popped it in my mouth without thinking. Yuck! The cafeteria was dark.

Where was Patty Anne? I got my answer before I had a chance to panic. She erupted out of the tray in a tidal wave of jello. I got gunked yet again. Patty Anne sputtered and coughed, trying to catch her breath.

She wiped her eyes and took a long look around. "Well, I guess you beat me to the finish line."

"Let's call it a tie." We both laughed.

Heavy footsteps echoed through the empty cafeteria. Lunch Lady Kuchen stomped out of the shadows, red-faced and scowling. Greasy hair poked out of her hairnet in odd places, and her uniform was even more blotchy than usual.

"What are you little brats doing in here at this time of the—" she barked. Then she got an eyeful of the mess we had made. Her face turned purple, and I swear I saw steam coming out of her ears.

She took a deep breath, like a train getting ready to blow her whistle. We stopped her with two big, gloppy hugs.

"Thank you for saving us!" I yelled.

"I am so happy to see you," Patty Anne said. I'm sure the two of us looked, and sounded, demented.

Mrs. Kuchen pushed us away with a disgusted look, then wiped her hands on her uniform. "I don't know what you're talking about. Patty Anne McGinty, I'm very disappointed in you. I thought you knew better than to get involved in this sort of destructive mischief. And you, Mr. Brannon. Well, I can't say I'm surprised, with your track record. And where's my creamed corn? Thanks to you, we ran out today!" So it was still the same day. Freaky.

Patty Anne and I looked at each other and shrugged. Lunch Lady Kuchen shook her head and snorted, like a bull having a bad day. "Get this slop cleaned up. I don't care how long it takes, it better be sparkling by tomorrow morning. And rest assured your parents will be receiving a call from me!" She gave us a final glare and walked away.

Yep, back to normal. "Come on, Patty Anne. I'll get the mop and you get the rags."

Patty Anne looked down at herself. "I'm going to be so grounded."

Mrs. Kuchen stopped at the door. "Hey Josh, Patty Anne," she called out. "Tomorrow we're having Tater Tots!"

She was turning away when I looked back, but I think I saw her wink.